Almarina

Valeria Parrella

Almarina

Translated by Alex Valente

JOHN MURRAY

First published in Italy in 2019 by Einaudi

First published in Great Britain in 2021 by John Murray (Publishers)
An Hachette UK company

This paperback edition published in 2022

3

This book has been translated thanks to a translation grant awarded by
the Italian Ministry of Foreign Affairs and International Cooperation.

Questo libro è stato tradotto grazie a un contributo alla traduzione assegnato
dal Ministero degli Affari Esteri e della Cooperazione Internazionale italiano.

A CIP catalogue record for this title is available from the British Library

Paperback ISBN 9781529352443
eBook ISBN 9781529352429

Typeset in Sabon MT by Hewer Text UK Ltd, Edinburgh
Printed and bound in Great Britain by Clays Ltd, Elcograf S.p.A.

John Murray policy is to use papers that are natural, renewable and
recyclable products and made from wood grown in sustainable forests.
The logging and manufacturing processes are expected to conform
to the environmental regulations of the country of origin.

John Murray (Publishers)
Carmelite House
50 Victoria Embankment
London EC4Y 0DZ

www.johnmurraypress.co.uk

'And I will give you news about a rosebush that I have planted and about a lizard that I want to train.'

Antonio Gramsci, *Letters from Prison*
(trans. Raymond Rosenthal)

Prologue

I'll never be able to tell if it's Naples or if it's me. If I suddenly feel the weight of it all because these last few days have been leaden, filled with fear and doubts, and suspicion. Or if it really is the sight of that eyesore of a building on the other side of the gate, the yellow wave rising, the domes beneath the clouds, beams too heavy for one woman to hold up. If in fact reality is a series of balconies out of reach, of powers out of reach, as they say; or if it's just us on one of those rare days when we wear our best clothes and set out on stairs leading to a different life.

The last time was barely three years ago, and the stairs were heading downwards as they led to a hospital morgue. Not just any hospital; it never could be after I found my husband there, his body cold on a slab of metal, his lips purple, his face as if doused in talcum powder.

It was only much later that I really started remembering the shape memories usually take: images, and a reconstruction of what we had said, and the sequence of things. I put everything in order then, but initially I only felt a trace of iron on my lips, as if I'd kissed the morgue's table and not Antonio's breathless mouth. I'd got there late, after everyone else was already in front of me: his sisters, set on being the first and foremost mourners then and thereafter, claiming the same monopoly they had in the past on much more trivial occasions. They'd arrived immediately as they shared his surname and had been contacted first; then they'd called me, called me again and again, and I didn't answer, just as I never answer most of life's crucial callings.

Because I teach at the Nisida youth detention centre, and my mobile phone rings in the security box at the entrance, as the rules dictate.

Each of us was where we had to be, while my husband's body with its exploded heart still in his chest had been carried from the pavement to the ambulance, from the ambulance to the hospital. Naples is a city that knows how to deal with death, giving it the same consideration as life: that is, taken individually, little more than nothing. And so, half an hour after the time of death (that was how the doctors – which doctors? – spoke), Antonio was in the morgue and I was walking down the steps that, whether I willed it or not, were about to change my life.

It's another April without him, the third one, and I'm walking briskly towards the youth courts beneath the pines of the Colli Aminei; something in the air suggests hope, and I find myself missing even my ugly sisters-in-law.

I have spent the past few days, the evenings, trying to fall asleep by piecing together my outfit in my mind. Lying still in bed, in the dark, as the house around me slowly cooled down, I wore jeans and jackets, then I chose a blouse; I tried the same jacket with some velvet trousers, then I fell asleep as I changed my shoes. (At night I must have dreamed about piercing my ears again.) I tried to give meaning to the day that awaited me with what I had: women dress up in celebration.

A courthouse is little more than a haphazardly assembled clinic, and much less than a well-assembled post office. Beyond the metal detector and the guards where you must show your summons there are dimly lit corridors, groups of people gathered at the windows all talking on their phones, the smell of cigarette smoke, crowded plastic chairs beneath neon lighting and numbers ticking down on a display. And there is a heavy atmosphere of doubt, pushing down on everyone's shoulders, carving out everyone's time. Time, that has so much value outside, is entirely worthless inside a waiting room: it becomes the foot frozen mid-step. It's unmovable, it'll last forever. In this forever, I've had my hair and nails done, and I scrape a piece of gum from the floor with my shoe. Although the guards in front of me have their guns covered by their jackets, I know them well, my eyes are trained to recognise prison roles, and an inmate is sitting between them, her posture showing all the signs of captivity. Defiant, bored, arrogant, submissive, trapped, fleeing. I can read the body language of inmates, just as students can spot a teacher in a middle-aged person on the tram. Society is divided into habitats and they gather into masses, the elements mimicing and resembling each other, subjected to the laws of probability. But then an individual leaves the class, rises from their condition and reverts to being unique, if just for a moment: 'I need to use the toilet,' the inmate says.

The toilets are a door to my left; the guard who stays outside holds open the door and the other does the same for the cubicle. The officer is a woman, she knows her stuff, she's confident and she doesn't look, she only holds her hand on the doorknob so the cubicle door can't shut. If she wanted to, she could watch the inmate crouched over the toilet. And we're all sitting here, waiting for our red number on the display, and the human condition clings to us and forces us to process that scene. We think of slave trades and migrants packed into cargo ships, Roman galleys, prison cells with no toilets, and Doctor Zhivago's still moving train when they need to empty the pail. The lawyer following my case calls to me, 'Come, it's our turn,' and I collect myself and head in.

I'll never be able to tell if everything actually was grey or if it was me; if the door really was made of grey laminate, the floor of grey resin and the window fixtures of grey aluminium; and if the faces of the committee at the back were also all grey. But the court was wide and lit by a beautiful arrangement of windows (though the sky outside was low, and Naples was absent), and the judges down there were all women, and so I said: 'Good morning.' Out loud, as I do when I walk into the classroom. I turned round to close the door and I saw her: Almarina.

I smiled at her, and I felt a sudden and complete relief. Almarina was looking at me from the corridor, and I understood why I was walking straight, keeping my elbows close to my body, and why my shoes were only one shade darker than my bag. Why I had spent so many nights getting dressed. I remembered the old-fashioned game of cardboard figures I would cut out with my cousins, when we were still young. Sitting on the steps of the house, while people inside were busy with chores, we coloured two-dimensional clothes that clung to our paper models with small paper tabs.

Memories always stay where you leave them: we get up, go inside, called to the dinner table by our mothers, and the memories stay out on the steps.

Almarina didn't have those kinds of memories and she had been the one dressed in paper, but the future shone in her eyes – and the future was starting now.

Almarina

My name is Elisabetta Maiorano, not that anyone asked. I'm the one reminding myself every time I reach the threshold of Nisida (just like I tell myself my card PIN as I walk up to the cash machine). I feel guilty every time I step inside. At the barrier, when I stop for identity checks, I need to lower my gaze, show my face without ever really looking the officer in the eye, as if my car were stuffed with cocaine. Then I see that barrier rise with incredible effort, as if I am the one who has to lift it, as if it is my fault that Nisida is a youth detention centre, as if I had dug out these streets of tuff with my own hands, forcing my car to struggle through them. As if they were doing me a favour.

Whenever I reach that barrier, I lose all civil rights, any substance I have accrued over time. I am no one, no longer a graduate or a qualified teacher who passed exams and spent years in temporary jobs up north and reacts badly to those trying to jump the queue. The person who reports the broken wing mirror or the keyed car door. ('Do you know who did it, madam?' 'Yes, I do: an illegal parking valet under San Pasquale, he wanted money and I told him I'd rather give it to a busker.' 'I'm afraid the busker may also have been illegal.')

At the corner of the Nisida guard lodge, I let them scrutinise me, but it's just my imagination, I tell myself: there are so many people heading out in the morning – educators, teachers, workshop facilitators – and my number plate is registered, and they never ask me anything really. They're posted here one day and who knows where next month, so maybe they don't even know that we're all climbing the mountain of purgatory, and that when we descend we will never be the same.

Elisabetta Maiorano. For the past three years I've been carrying my passport instead of my national ID card, as my passport doesn't have my marital status and my card still says *married* and I have no desire to pay a visit to the General Register Office to get it changed.

(There was a lot of dust making the whole atmosphere not entirely believable as I was applying for my national ID: a little ironic. The clerks were indistinguishable from ordinary citizens, or maybe not: they looked more worn out, wearing jumpers that would never come back into fashion.

'Can't we just put *not applicable* under marital status and employment status?' 'Lady, if you don't want to let people know you're married, just use your passport.'

I hadn't been quick enough to respond, or laugh. It takes me a while to understand fully what is happening to me, I'm quicker to act than to think and I just left in frustration. Then, when I became a widow, the suggestion turned out to be useful.)

As the barrier closes behind me, I feel freer. I've received a glance to let me pass, I've overcome the otherwise uncrossable threshold, and for the first stretch I feel relief. Relief from everything. If only you knew what it means being able to turn around for a moment, on the stretch of road just before the turn. Stopping as the body continues, changes gear, plays with the clutch, prepares the wheel for the turn, as the body rises; finding yourself beyond the barrier and not yet at the prison, leaving the whole city below with its anxieties, which are also my own. If only you knew, as you walk down the huge roads, as you pray in the church of site E in the central district next to the courts of law. As you're spending your holidays, as you've just finished giving your talk at the convention, I want to call your attention to the west, make you turn around, and tell you that the anguished woman ascending to Nisida is not an inmate. She's a fifty-year-old woman and she married late, for a number of reasons but mostly because she had travelled a lot to stand in for other teachers. She has been to Treviso, has learned to drink white wine in the morning, to drive in the snow. She has learned to kill time, to dance the tango in Frosinone; she has helped the custodial staff hang up a sheet at the weekend to use as a screen for a film projection. And when she got back, it was very late indeed.

But that's not the point either. The point is that before she gets to the prison and when already beyond the barrier, if you look closely, you can see it: she's feeling a strange kind of relief. Maybe people used to travelling feel the same thing when the plane takes off. The only things taking off here are a few seagulls, and a rock that rises like a pinnacle just as the road swerves. All else is silence. The silence you can never hear elsewhere: away from the sailing routes, far from any road, inaccessible sea all around, diving into Vesuvius on the right and into the Italsider plant on the left. But today everything is idle, including the volcano and the steelworks.

The moment of comforting relief lasts for the turn in the road and then I'm already faced with the pottery buildings, the workshops. Inside the barrier but still outside the prison, in the cold morning, the cold air, I am the car boot weighed down by a life of labour. I see the kids in their hoods, in their jackets, smoking by the side of the road. I don't remember their faces, I don't recognise any of them when they wave hello: a car, a teacher, a dog, you always wave hello to a guest. I recognise their roles: these are the 'article 21s', people on day release who only need return at night. Inside the same institution there are different circles to which inmates belong, to the point of adopting its name. They form spontaneously, unspoken, relative to the type of imprisonment, the length of the sentence, how long they've been inside, the way they behave. The 'fourth wing' are the ones who can eat in their room without having to attend the refectory. The article 21s are looking at me through the windscreen, and I need to act under their watchful eyes. I can't let the car stall, I need to find a spot immediately, I need to park. I need to be competent, because they're looking at me and their judgement wears me out.

I choose the low parking area, the furthest away and probably the emptiest. And here is a new truce, rising from a patch of shade cast by the Posillipo promontory on to Vesuvius, hiding one of its humps. And from the fact that, across all that water, down there, you can see Capri. Capri is a place where everyone is well, tourists take the cable car, stopping in the tiny piazza. Foreigners live there all year round, their kids in high schools speak English, Russian, Ancient Greek; four steaks are 150 euros. Capri shows its best side in winter: it's clear to see, even from here. And I need to leave my phone behind soon, and it won't be my fault.

As I walk towards the bulletproof glass, I feel I will finally cast aside the ropes mooring me to this weary life I've ended up with. It's the rules, my hands are tied: for the next five hours it will not be down to me and just like everyone entering Nisida I will be free again, a child again.

The guard asks my name and surname, surly, unsmiling, not inviting at all. Other times, other days, better guards, one more smile.

My name is Elisabetta Maiorano. I think somewhere in my past there must have been some kind of royal ambition. The only thing I inherited, in the end, is a shoebox full of silverware. I was preparing for an exam, living in pyjamas most of the time and I regularly slipped through the courtyard of statues, reappearing in the university library. As I was photocopying something, as I wore my desert boots, as it rained in via Mezzocannone, thieves broke into my student house and that box was the only thing they didn't take.

('It was Gypsies: Gypsies hate silver,' said my neighbour, with no trace of doubt.

And the police: 'Why are you living alone?'

'Why is that any of your business?')

They hand me a key that fits a locker. I make a pouch out of my bag, I punch it, squash it, make it fit, I turn the key and leave. I leave inside the locker the solitude of the only child, the pain in the ear of an illness-induced eruption, the shadow cast over the wall of my bedroom that terrified me in the afternoons. The answer I snapped back that caused my mother to stop talking to me for days. Their hands still over you when you don't really want them, wanting more hands on you and not being able to ask. The first panic attack in a hotel room in Paris, after leaving school. And the holiday with a man older than me, during which I cried every day.

And still after I got dressed this morning, after braving the cold in my house, I hid the bags under my eyes with a line of concealer, brushed my hair upside down. I did it because the students would study me, so that the girls could see something familiar in me, something they hone in their cells. So that the boys would see the image of a woman they respect. But these are all entirely my ideas, and who knows where respect actually comes from. I'm not talking about them, I don't know anything about them. I'm talking about me. About how I prop myself up to avoid death. When I looked at myself in the mirror I saw a tired woman. An old tired woman with a raging hangover who is unable to hold the mascara because crying comes more naturally to her than make-up. An old woman, so I wasn't thinking about having carried all that childhood to stuff into the cupboard.

The guards at the entrance are as impenetrable as their office. They've never been rude, just enough breath to say good morning. There's something soviet about their eyelids, something to defend themselves against me and against the Ural winds. Sometimes they ask for ID. Others check your name on a list: ELISABETTA MAIORANO. Who am I? What's my purpose here? Am I a threat to the incarcerated minors? Am I a threat to myself? What am I planning, where am I going? Other times: 'The lockers are full.' And so you have to head back to the car and leave everything in the glove compartment.

To go through the main gate you have to ring a bell, about ten short steps from the guard who checked my ID. But that's protocol: I reach the gate, ten short steps later, and I have to ring as if I just got here. The same guard who checked my ID, ten short steps earlier, opens the gate.

There's a different atmosphere in this process, between the guards and the gate, one of rarefied oxygen. It's the same feeling found in the waiting rooms of public offices, the same generated by the screens compiling the results of your mammogram. It's the same atmosphere exhaled from tax collection envelopes, which speeds up your heart rate as you're in the bank signing papers. The pull of gravity increases, makes your feet heavier, and you start heaving in over-saturation of carbon dioxide.

The gate slides on its track, and it reveals the light within: even if it's raining, there's always more light than where I've come from. I have nothing, it's just me in my clothes, and if I have something I need to get or take to play with it has to be with me already, in my chromosomes, in what I will say, in what I know, in the way I'll raise my eyes and what and where I'll look. There's this long stretch on foot, a walk by the volleyball court, bordered on the left by the women's wing, with its large flowerpots next to the steps, always impeccably kept. Flowerpots and flowers, not flowerpots and cigarettes. And then there's the long yellow mural. So I'm free in the time it takes to walk this stretch, inside the walls, beyond the gate, before the inmates, pockets empty. I'm me, and no one can do anything about it. Husband who passed away you can do nothing, city you can do nothing, sisters-in-law vacuuming under the bed, you can do nothing about it.

It's early, the courtyards are empty, the geese are alone in the pet therapy coop. And there are these young men, dressed in dark colours. Long femurs inside denim, trained legs: tall men who remind me of better days when I hadn't learned to look. Times when youth meant good looks and I couldn't see it that clearly. Faced with bodies like that, at their age, I wouldn't have known what to do. It's a little better now, a little different, but only thanks to them: they look at me, and when you look you're starting a game. So you straighten your shoulders, puff your chest out, look ahead, curl part of your lips in a smile. More guards. They're in their thirties, radios in hand, keys attached to the loops of their jeans, something seductive in their gait. They greet me without too much familiarity; I don't know every one of them, maybe they all know me and that's all that matters. If I'm there it means I'm authorised to be there. I am the one transfigured as I pass them, I'm the one looking to see if they're smoking, and hoping that a woman may appear among them one day. I'm the one with the idea that guards are cops, and cops are bad, and that you're guilty because as soon as you meet one a stone is born in your pocket. How can we both be inside Nisida if I've chosen to be a teacher and you chose to be a prison guard? If you believe in repression, why am I looking for your approval? And you don't even ask me where I'm going, as I head towards the workshops.

'Professor Maiorano.' He heads my way swiftly, dynamic gait, really dark eyes. 'Dr Maiorano, I need to ask you, I really do: did someone from your family use to teach at the Della Porta?'

'Yes, my granddad Luigi, he taught Italian.'

'You look just like him, your granddad but with curly hair. Imagine! Is he still around?'

'Ah, no, he died in the 90s . . . Were you one of his students?'

'Maronna, teach, who could forget him, he'd put us through the mill every day, he was a *carabiniere* your granddad.'

'Was he strict?'

'He was very well trained, of course, but his behaviour, his methods . . . a different time, know what I mean?'

'What do you mean?'

'I mean, can I say it? Your grandad was a fascist, we would occupy the school, we even smashed his car window once. He was the enemy, that's how you think when you're that age. Have some coffee, I haven't touched it . . .'

'Please, you first, I'm wearing lipstick.'

'I insist, come on. Unbelievable, your granddad's face with curly hair . . .'

There's a new girl in class today.

'Fortunately, a judge sent her here,' says my colleague, the one who teaches literature and Italian.

She tells us she's sixteen years old, she's Romanian (what is left of her anyway, after her father's violence, sexual and physical).

'What's your name?'

'Almarina.'

Her father broke some bones, I'm not sure which: perhaps important bones, part of her spine, ribs, a kneecap.

There's a place in your head where the worst thoughts, those we never usually admit to having, not only enter but obediently queue up to do so. And as I look at her, my obediently queued-up thought says: I can understand hating a child to the point of killing them, but I can't understand raping them. (Do I really understand? Is that the word?) The new student's hand is stiff as it holds the pen, making her look like one of those old chain-smoking women ruined by arthritis. Now I need to sit in front of her and see if she understands basic maths. Which means I need to sit in front of her and wait for that hand to draw a line on the page, dividing the factors from the result.

'Can you speak Italian?'

'Yes.'

On the page is this man who rapes her and breaks her ribs, her father. And a brother. A brother who was six years old when she brought him with her to Italy.

'Shall we try multiplication? Do you want to? 35×68. No, switch those, look: always put the highest number at the top.'

The nail of my index finger, coated with the cheap polish I bought yesterday, is so close to the mark of her pen, to her misshapen hand, that it brushes against the hold of the lorry she travelled in with her brother. She paid for the journey herself on the lorry, every time, any time they wanted. Wait, 5×8 = 40, move it there, put it underneath or you'll get lost. So her brother is around somewhere. The brother who arrived with her. They find them in Fano and separate them: he goes to a foster home and she goes to a centre. She must have felt so grown up when they took him to safety. Maybe she thought he was being adopted, as do the Annunziata mothers when they lay their babies on the foundling wheel at night.

You need to add those. Addition. Plus sign.

She doesn't remember calculations; she never attended classes at the centre. How is that possible? I don't look into it. ('Elisabè, what can I say? Her greatest crime was stealing a phone.' 'Really?' 'Yeah, which means the judge sent her here.')

In these cases we usually trace the steps back all the way to the starting point, the one we know about: there must be a moment, a home, a day, the warmth of a bed somewhere inside all this. Addition. She knows addition, so we'll start with the terms and the sum, the substitution property.

Lessons don't last long, the guards come to call the girls and when she stands up she's only a little taller than when she was sitting down. She's a knot, a ball of thread, a monkey in a lumpy acetate jumpsuit and she heads off.

At this point, there are some things that need saying. For example, one of the things we can say is 'almost time to head out again and back to our lives' (and I don't like this one because life outside is bitter). Or 'I'll bring her a book on Frida Kahlo tomorrow, simple writing, lots of coloured pictures. I wonder where I put it.'

Later, the captain's dog will come towards me. It's big, a wolf, one of those used by cops to sniff out drugs in airports. It eats biscuits, breadsticks, sweets and everything that the kids can carry from the prison supplies, from the packages they get from their families, from what's left over from their midnight feasts, from the times when their blood sugar crashes. It grazes on crumbs out of their hands and then dreams of devouring the pet therapy geese. The dog will lead me to the volleyball court, where the captain has set up a match.

Watching them now, they look like students in a PE class. Some of them have more expensive shoes than you'd expect, some would never wear those clothes at school, but the rules on this blue rectangle are the same everywhere: as long as you're in the blue rectangle you win if you score points and the others lose. The roles change. The girls with long nails are losing, the boys who care about their hair don't dive and aren't any use to anyone, the power dynamics flip, the sport's aesthetic does not match what they watch on TV in the evening in their cells. Under the net, on the other side, I see the Romanian girl again.

The Romanian girl is good, she serves well, she rushes to defend the point. The Romanian girl is generous, her teammates look to her, consult her. The captain leaves the court in a T-shirt even though it's December and he comes towards me. We say a few things, I even reply, but I don't focus on him: I'm watching a Romanian girl hitting over the net, almost flying. He notices, tilts his head to share my gaze. The captain knows everything and his knowing everything annoys me; how dare he use his intuition to read what I'm thinking!

'If the Romanian girl can fly, it's me who's the idiot,' I'm thinking, and he knows and I know that I'll never tell him, because I see him as my inferior and superior at the same time.

This is Nisida's decalibration: once I step inside I have to readjust constantly, reposition myself, watch my back and look inside myself, then make a level-headed judgement.

The captain is an officer of the prison staff, but we all just call him the captain. And because Nisida is a vessel and his eyes are blue, every now and then he dives down and fishes, diving deep and bringing back something for us when he resurfaces. Today was a mixed genders volley-ball match, and even the dog played its part as it hates the ball to touch the ground. The match becomes real once everyone starts enjoying themselves, when they all become children again, young children. It won't last, but as long as childhood wonder is there, you can see it.

It's in this space that the captain and I are peers: two proud parents at the side of the court, a woman and a man watching the liquid flow of responsibility all around. The captain knows that these kids are much younger than us and will be alive and travelling the world when we're dead; even if their sentence were to last twenty years, they'll still leave here younger than we are now. And if they don't live on after us, it'll be because death followed them down the alley, gun in hand.

The captain is wearing his T-shirt tucked into his jeans and no weapons, because they're not allowed here.

But there was a day when his father, or someone acting for him, bought an official gazette and signed him up for an exam. We had just finished secondary school, maybe it was the same month I went to Paris for the first time. We'd dreamed of it, the Paris of books and films, we'd dreamed of it along Naples' roads, leaving school, swarming on to via Foria. It was one of those small dots on the horizon that allow you to keep a steady course.

Inside the Père-Lachaise metro at night, serious, focused on the directions, a few francs to spend a day and every train leaving could take us so far away. Seen from there, our city was a ragged cousin, even Rome never felt like a capital. We lived among Bourbon glories we never knew and we all wanted to lose ourselves and never meet up again. There, beneath Père-Lachaise, with Paris streaming over our heads in the June of our final exams, life had prospects. If anyone had asked, we would've labelled it with a lower-case letter of the alphabet, like you do with lines in geometry: a line with no beginning and no end. Those same nights in June the captain could clearly see the segment ascribed to him: point A was printed in front of his eyes, 'OJ 4th Special Series – Exams for 13–06–1988'. Point B was where he was now standing with me, thirty years later, at the side of the court, sturdy, life-loyal to his faith, wedding ring on his finger, two almost grown-up children.

He came to Antonio's funeral with his wife. The service was something I remembered badly, replied to a priest I didn't recognise, putting in their mouths something that reminded me of the ancient Farmacia degli Incurabili. My sisters-in-law had packaged, in barely twenty-four hours, a day that brought everyone together, when even the captain and his wife could come and pay their respects; they'd been right, basically. But more importantly, something had happened that I had kept to myself and which, because of the blasphemy it contained, paid me back for the religious swiftness of that couple of church ladies. Every time I looked up towards the captain, he was looking at me. Not the priest, nor the dark coffin in the centre of the aisle, nor the altar, nothing but me. What he was thinking about didn't matter, what happened to me every time I met his eyes was that the pain in my heart felt a little lighter, just for a moment, then it would swoop back to the inevitability of death. That look meant 'I'm here for you, I didn't even know your husband' and 'I'm here, no matter what.' And 'I'll carry the memory of this pain into Nisida as long as I have to so you won't be alone.'

With time, after that first year, when my appetite had come back and my desire to go out into the street, one night even my lust returned. And so I brought that look under the sheets. The captain as a person, his reality, had nothing to do with it. I was the one to move a compassionate look into an erotic sphere, to take the day and move it into the night, with all its contradictions, power plays, the roles it contained – and that scared me. With the weight of judgement, even because of that weight, with a gaze fixed upon me I had come back to life, by myself.

The girls go in first, then the boys. In sections, staggered, slowly called back to the workshops. There are rules in Nisida, which are the same ones kids on the outside follow, those who won't end up in Nisida. They have to go to school, they really have to, they must. School is the only space without bars on the windows. The guards search the boys as soon as they step out of the door, a procedure that has always shocked me, and so I look away. (When I was small, my father used to say you shouldn't look at people who are fighting, limping or drunk. Not looking at people living in a different situation to your own was middle-class training.)

The girls are chatting on the way in, they greet me without looking at me, but Almarina smiles at me and she opens her eyes wide. She's waiting to see what happens now. She thinks I can give her the feeling she needs, or that's what I think, which is the same as a relationship.

Except that I am terrified to death, while Almarina shoves her fear under her broken shoes and watches me, fixed in her present. She's there, right there, waiting to know if it's geometric shapes or flowers. I'm the one who has to give, they just take and take and take.

If I sit next to her now and not in the middle, I'm going too far. If I take Pythagoras's theory and force myself to ignore the request, I'm not doing enough.

Almarina hands me her hope and I do wrong.

But it can't be refused. When you step in here you can no longer say no to anything, Nisida's inmates don't ask permission to treat you badly or well. There used to be a girl sitting in front of me for years, until age took her to rot her menstruation in who knows what cell: her eyes broken like frogs in winter. Another, instead, held her guilt for her crime in her gaze like a horse with its yoke. Their crimes can be described in two sentences, and they can't speak them, not even to us teachers. They're stories murmured in the staffroom while we heat up coffee on the small electric hob. And when our literature colleague tells us, we listen and we look at each other without pity or anger, disappointment or horror, without solidarity for the victims or the perpetrators. We just take these files and archive them deep in our memories and then we hide the keys. Our hope, I think, is that on that distant day when everyone will have served their sentence, the key will be back in their hands, and white sheets of paper will fly out of our open archives, no more ink on them, just pure white, like laundry hung up to dry on our balconies.

But no one understands this, because to understand it you need to see it. And who really wants to see something like this?

So I rummage deep in my pockets to find whatever is left, and I find my grandmother.

My grandmother used to teach maths. She loved maths, she'd see it everywhere: in the tension holding up the dome of Donnaregina vecchia, in the wait for the tram along the main road, in her hands as she weighed the spaghetti, one hundred grams each exactly.

I have nothing to give you, Romanian girl, I'm just getting by, do you see that? Everything I have I stole for myself thirty years ago, when I lived in my grandmother's house and I'd pinch fifty thousand liras from her retirement every week. Twenty years of infinitesimal calculus to avoid losing my mind. Everything that followed has been passive income from that effort, from that will of youth, of tears poured over textbooks on mathematical analysis. I'm getting by, Romanian girl.

I'm only five minutes late, even though I drank too much and I took some drops in order to sleep, and I'm believable. Because I'm at work, my dear, you're not. I have a bank account and no one can take it away. And I go swimming at lido Elena in summer. I can, Romanian girl, and this is my job.

No flowers today, just geometric shapes.

A few days later, she fell asleep on her desk. We were learning about operations between fractions. We needed to draw a long line and find the least common multiple among the denominators. And she'd fallen asleep, and I only noticed because her classmates were laughing about it. So I asked her why she hadn't slept the previous night.

She told me she didn't know, maybe she was praying – she always heard a low, constant litany in a mysterious language at night.

Before the boys could do anything, I turned towards them, shielding her with my person. And I didn't kill them with my eyes only because I was unarmed. I knew that they could've woken her up at any second, yelling, and if they'd noticed that I cared about her that would've motivated them to do it even more. I decided that shouldn't happen and I even had time to realise that I was ready to attempt any trick in the book. Unassign work, give them really good marks, end the lesson early, give out cigarettes. The boy I was most afraid of, childish and always rowdy, was sentenced to the blackboard with the prime numbers table. He stood up and threw his chair to the ground, but Almarina was sleeping with her face in her elbow. All of the others were to copy from the blackboard. All of them. Prime numbers are like other numbers: infinite. (Up to three digits, if I don't actually know them, I can at least guess.) I sentenced the girl with the best voice, the one who's always singing, to read them out loud one by one from the book. (Sooner or later they'll notice that they don't have to be paying attention to the blackboard, and Almarina will wake up. They never noticed.)

Everything was normal: through the glass door the guards could see a student writing numbers and the others copying them. The teacher leaning against a desk, watching the classroom. Inside her: the teacher loading up on natural remedies for anxiety. she can't find warmth in her bed not even in may. her arm hurts and it's a heart attack.

her belly hurts and it's appendicitis. it's not bad enough to call the neighbours but not even normal enough to sleep through it. she hates that night in october because it's back to daylight saving and when it's finally three it goes back to two. she keeps the television on as long as the programming is live, she's terrified of repeats. she peers at the window and sees the light of a cigarette from a balcony: so someone else is awake. she needs a crack of light. she needs to hear the car engines as they drive by. her spinning head is an earthquake, but the sweat is definitely menopause (her husband used to say 'you could never get the menopause, maybe a menogoes,' but now the husband has gone and reaching out with her foot does nothing). it's so great to get up to pee and it's already 5 a.m., sunrise is in an hour: something in the air tells her she's made it, she's alive, she finally falls asleep.

The inmates are rowdy now, they're throwing things, asking to leave, no one is copying from the blackboard any more and the teacher has to rein them in, but Almarina sleeps and inside her the maths teacher finally falls asleep. And then it's time to go (there is no bell here ringing its freedom trill, the hours are not hours). The guards come in, Almarina wakes up and her cheek has the mark of the Madonna del Buon Consiglio – a silver pendant that her grandmother gave her.

Florian is tall and skinny, he wears a plastic apron when he heads into the geese coop. He's fun, he's always in a good mood; there is nothing in him of the malaise that rises from the gutters of the city. He is not shifty or malicious, never an improper gesture. All covered in mud he looks like he just stepped out of a Flemish painting: prison has restored a northern origin to him that Naples had dulled.

'The geese feel the cold, Professor.'

I step into the yard as the captain's dog growls with envy.

'You know what Miss Aurora told me? There was this German philosopher who looked after geese. Can you believe it, Professor?'

'I don't know, I know about the scientist who worked with mules.'

'A vet?'

'No, an astronomer, he led the mules up and down Mount Wilson as the Americans were building the largest observatory of all time. His name was Humason, he was fourteen years old and whenever he reached the top there was this girl who'd make him lose his head over her.'

'What was her name, Professor?'

'I don't know, she was the daughter of one of the observatory's designers.'

'Big cheese.'

'A famous architect, he didn't like the idea of this kid as a son-in-law.'

'And did they manage to get together anyway?'

'I'm getting there, in the end the observatory was ready, and poor Humason lost his job. So he started doing anything he could to stay on Mount Wilson. He began working as an assistant electrician.'

'They had electricity already, Professor?'

'Yes, since 1882. Then he became a security guard, then he started cleaning the dome, because you need spanking clean glass to be able to study the stars.'

'They never slept?'

'There were staff all night, taking photos with the telescope.'

'They already had photography, Professor?'

'Heavens, yes, since 1850, anyway one night the technician in charge of photos was ill, and they searched and searched and searched and the only person left up on Mount Wilson was Humason.'

'Did he know astronomy, Professor?'

'Not at all, he never even wanted to go to school, but he was a quick learner and that night he took photos so precise that they were better than the technician's, so the astronomers appointed him as the photographer.'

'Nice. And the girl?'

'Hang on.'

'If you say hang on it means there's a happy ending, Professor . . .'

'On one happy day a new director is appointed, the greatest American astronomer, Hubble. Hubble talks to the mule herd and sees he's got potential and he starts teaching him science and astronomy. So Humason starts having all these ideas and begins working with Hubble and what did they discover? That galaxies are moving: the further they are from Earth, the more they move, and what does this mean?'

'. . .'

'That the universe isn't still, it moves, because one day,

billions of years ago, our universe was born from an explosion, and the bits of that explosion are still travelling. Basically, Humason discovered the origin of our universe.'

'God didn't make the universe, Professor?'

'No.'

'And the girl?'

'They married.'

'Knew it.'

'And there's a comet and an asteroid both called Humason up there.'

'So what did God do, Professor?'

'There is no God.'

'You're wrong Professor. God is the whole of this story you've told me.'

The smell arrives with no warning, carried by the wind, and it takes a few seconds to recognise. It's sulphur, coming from inland, coming from the Astroni crater or around there. Maybe it happens in the evening, when the wind blows from the land, or maybe it happens when we're ready to see ourselves in the land. It's a strong smell that rises from the centre of the planet, comes from afar and opens up your lungs. It's not a reassuring sight like the Carmine bell tower, the San Martino vineyard, Punta della Campanella after the rain. It's not something you can chase, leaning as you look for it, when you need to ground yourself in the moment. Because it's a smell that arrives without warning, and it can either be there or not, afternoon or morning, for a minute or until nightfall. It arrives, and when it does it's a relief, a gift from the Sybil, bearing the shape of a premonition and a memory.

The first time I saw Antonio it was dusk. We'd staggered in and then, once inside the Solfatara, we'd split into groups. The September hour, that night in our thirties, was beautiful.

'But he's married, he's wearing a ring,' my colleague had said.

'No, I mean the other one.'

Then, walking along the ridge, the soles of our shoes growing warm and the continuous voice of the geologist invoking disasters, we giggled and moved closer.

I was marrying the one of the two who wasn't messing around. That's what my colleague would say in City Hall, acting as a witness to my wedding. Do you, Elisabetta Maiorano? Because she'd spent all night with the seducer, who made her laugh, while Antonio and I were on that moon landscape: brushing the borders of silver craters. looking at our hands in disbelief. perceiving in one go the horizon, vanished from the centre of the volcano. don't be afraid, at all.

'Nothing bad could ever come from here, to me,' I told him, convinced, and maybe he thought I was trying to prove the geologist wrong, and that trust isn't always well placed anyway.

'You've been here already?'

'Yes, when I was university. You?'

'When I was younger, with my parents.'

(We were wearing velvet, maybe we looked the same, me, mum and dad holding hands, flared trousers and jumpers with wooden buttons or long cable patterns running all the way down, scratching the skin on our chins. They took me to the Cave of Dogs, and told me that it was called that because if dogs went inside it they'd never come out alive. I learned that carbon dioxide crawls low on the ground, I thought about the elements, about the fact that heavier molecules live at lower strata, and I decided I'd be studying science.)

Twenty years later, as my colleague and the seducer were cooking anchovies, laughing in the way that signals intent, I headed into the darkness. 'Come,' I told the man I was letting myself be accompanied by into my memory. We were careful, we knew that lakes of boiling mud don't spare even those who know them, that the sudden burst of a geyser can scar you forever. But the Cave of Dogs was out of bounds: the volcano was walking all around us. We didn't kiss that night, nor the times after that: there was no rush now that we had met. We proceeded with the care given to things eternal.

At dawn, when I cross the empty and rarefied city, it shines. I cross its beautiful streets in my car, the closed metal shutters belonging to good shops that will only open three hours later. We head on in the meantime, we are the people of the early cafés and those stepping off trams, until you turn on to the promenade from piazza Vittoria, just behind Castel dell'Ovo, and the sun is rising. It starts as a light lens only finding its circumference as it's mirrored on the sea. It's white, and I have it in my mirror, while in my windscreen Posillipo is a pink hill.

The city before it's a city is mine alone and it's how I want it. It saved my life: to avoid missing it I tear away from the clasp of the sheets, the chemistry that protects me and pins me down for hours. I brave the empty house, the memory of naked feet on Antonio's socks: 'I'm cold, carry me to the bathroom,' then an unstable robot trip with his arm beneath my breasts.

It wasn't just that. There were fights, and yelling, and promises of break-ups, and shit belonging to others that we flung as if it were our own. Small satchels of shit brought home from the past like ammo. It was also not fucking for a month and me being suspicious of him and he suspicious of me.

A single cup on the morning table is not reason enough to wake up. But Naples is.

I enter the Piedigrotta tunnel and as I'm under there – exhausts, car lights, break lights, someone overtaking me on the wrong side – above me is Leopardi's tomb and a rectangular stone I saw many years ago saying that Virgil is also buried there.

('Who cares if it's true,' said the boy who'd taken me to see it; we were there to kiss, not for the dead, nor for poetry.)

Every day I take it I'm surprised that the tunnel holds and allows us to travel through the underworld to the other side, allowing us to reach Fuorigrotta, return to our lives, idling with our windows up and the windscreen wipers outside. As the lights turn yellow we all feel the relief of being among peers – all the same, all servants to clockwork time.

*

It's cold in the classroom, we bring in heaters and cheap blankets sold in supermarkets, ugly but warm. I position the heater towards my feet and I place myself in between the desks to explain square roots, paper and pen. I do everything in my head and everything on paper, me on paper, interpreter of ancient rules. I simplify for them the symbols that were traced for me in the severe university classroom.

Us up above everything, at the top of the steps, looking down at the professor who would be life or death, the master of our sleeping hours. The day of the exam, heading to the toilets to gain some extra time, hearing a coursemate say 'she was here just now,' then 'it's your turn.' Even those who have experienced a warm classroom have known the instinct to run, but each of us ended up learning those symbols and now I must filter it all for them. Avoid the inaccessible ones, favour the useful ones, and come up with a way of teaching them. I rarely bring a textbook with me, but they don't fear it when I do: they hold on to it, and the abyss of the unknown it contains.

The girls are less excited, less defiant. If they get distracted it's not because they don't value the lesson, but rather because of the hormones stalking their blood, making them broil with wants and beauty. Even in rags, because it's rags they're wearing. They don't have the boys' shiny shoes, the high-end gifts of the Camorra, but maybe three changes of clothes, synthetic fibres, jumpers all the same size, all with the same lack of shape. And then they smile, and inside the mouths that can't keep quiet they have flowers that overpower you. The girls are restless.

So I took Almarina's arm and I pulled with two fingers at the thin sleeve covering it – 'How are you not cold?' – and when I did, I felt a knot under the material. A hard spot that didn't belong to a human being, almost grooved wood, or a hook. That was the first time I touched her.

She looked at me with pity, she pitied me, I was the naive one, born yesterday and almost pulling back; I had really thought we were all born equal.

I couldn't ask. Maybe the other inmates did it. But those of us outside can never be inside and so we're never really made aware. I wanted to ask, but just to ask, no morbidity, not as doctor or priest.

Instead she looked at me and smiled, she brushed aside the papers filled with exponents and bases in front of her and pulled her sleeve up.

It was a ploughed field in winter.

Halfway down, between her wrist and elbow, was a ditch. I plunged my finger into it. I found frozen mud, half her face buried in it, the eye from the other half is following a boy running up a hill, and watching him go is sweet, a comforting thought to distract from the beating. The other thought is: when I get up from here I'll run away and you'll never see me again. There's a lorry, a trip into the mountains, a bit of snow falling even though it's October. There's a man in front who lets you understand that you can travel only if you take his thing in your mouth, and anyway your front teeth were left in the mud like in that story with the dragon. And what if one day from every planted tooth a woman rises, a giant woman?

*

Bird's-eye view of Almarina: she fights with her cellmate and she only wins because her hair is short and Kadija can't pull it. But it's all show: you can see their hearts aren't in it, and the others immediately jump in to pull them apart.

Side view of Almarina: she prays every night, cross-legged on her bed, while in front of the window Kadija writes fiery letters with her lighter. May the boys' wing read them.

Back view of Almarina: she checks the sourdough lumps rising for pizza. 'They've grown,' she says, as if they were alive, and so they are.

Close-up view of Almarina: her face has a doubtful smirk, and you won't wipe it off her.

Almarina out of view thinks of her mother, whose outlines are the stuff of dreams. (In her dreams she tells her off or hugs her, or she's in another room, but she's there.) She was. She can't make sense of the fact that the life she remembers is the same she's living now: the death of her mother, the loss of her brother, not being able to see the black woods, the snow. Which is why it hurts so much when an inmate is transferred, or even comes to the end of their sentence: Almarina knows that what can't be seen no longer exists.

It's the same for us: seeing them leave is the hardest thing, because where will they go? They're still so young, and they'll be going back to where they came from, and where they came from is the reason they're here. Or maybe they're older, and so they'll go to a different prison that isn't this one, that doesn't float off the coast of the involuntary city.

This mother cannot remember all of her children, she has too many, some are saved, others drown, others kill their siblings or starve them: those are the laws of nature and the bigger the city the more nature increases its odds and wins.

Nisida is out there, moored. We come and go. They come and go. I've seen come and go so many temporary staff and teachers who had asked for literally anything so that they could be transferred somewhere closer. I've seen young intelligent priests lead Mass and hand out Hosts, or baptise tiny Romani girls, daughters of small Romani girls who as long as they stay here won't get pregnant again.

Generous judges often refer to this structure as a foster home, as if it were a home. A home is a place where you eat and stay warm and you learn to walk unknown streets without being afraid of each other, carrying a lot of respect for yourself. They come here as children: children have no awareness of time and they tell you that seven years of prison is a number that means nothing, marked in wax on a birthday cake, if they ever got one. They've never assigned a notch of their life to each candle. And so they pick a guard, one of those with kind eyes who never did anything to them, they pick that one and they call them over to empty their bin, then they attack them and steal their keys and it's chaos. They get another seven years. Seven plus seven is fourteen and it's all the same to them.

If any number is the same as its double, that's zero.

Social workers come and go, stay forever or run away, relieved as soon as the promontory becomes a distant image in their rear-view mirror. It's not the barrier, it's not the armoured gate, it's not the bulletproof glass. It's Alice's door that diminishes or emboldens you, depending on how you go through it. Depending on how well you resist the frustration of being useless. Or on how capable you are of convincing yourself that you can be useful. Accepting a new classroom every day, never finishing a syllabus because there is no syllabus, just like in some schools in the countryside about a hundred years ago, when a single teacher had to do everything from basic literacy to at least basic numeracy, a result of school reform taking people away from the fields. One day you'll have no girls, one day no boys, and one day that one kid who did so well in maths will be gone and never come back. And yet, the night before, I had marked just one mistake on one line, but the judge transferred him yesterday afternoon. And I'll be here with his test, without ever hearing from him, I'll file it in his records somewhere, a memory of young shoulders hunched over the lined paper, and if I met him outside I wouldn't recognise him. And in any case, he wouldn't call to me to greet me.

It finally happened: I found Almarina on the bench, her knees huddled into her chest. They were playing that unbalanced game in front of her, with the dog as ball boy and at least eight players per side. I was leaving, the volleyball court is the last thing on your left as you exit Nisida. And if you leave during game time, it's sweeter.

You just have to not look at them when you go, and you have to go, by law, and they have to stay by law. This separation is inhuman. A fierce tear which should warrant us prison teachers at least double the pay, or as our English colleague says, at least a state-funded plastic surgeon. And there she was, on the last bench before the world, huddled up. So I sat next to her.

'Are you okay?'

'I've got my period.'

'Don't you want a painkiller?'

'I'm not saying it hurts, I'm saying the Virgin Mary sent me my period again.'

'You think the Virgin Mary had periods? Anyway, were you worried you might be pregnant?'

'Not pregnant, no, I haven't had it for two years.'

'Elephant pregnancies last two years.'

'I haven't had it since they took the baby from my belly.'

'An abortion?'

'Yes, with the lady, my grandma took me.'

'Not a hospital? Did it hurt?'

'No it wasn't like a hospital, it was the lady's house, it hurt but then it stopped.'

'Did you want to keep it?'

'No, no, it was against nature, you see? It was after . . . No, I couldn't have.'

And I understood, perfectly, but maybe they don't know how much we teachers know, how many details.

It's just that we go through such efforts to explain the syllabus to the kids, or to make them think about normal things, good things, as you'd do with any kid you care for.

It's a pedagogical notion yet to be enshrined in theory, the way in which we sweeten reality, tell it a little less harshly. So in here we always ask the girls about love stories, we admire the hairdo they've managed after shampooing with whatever tools they can scrape together. Always like this, for years: denominators and nail polish, farmers selling apples and compliments on the pottery tiles coming out of the kilns.

I know that inmates sometimes talk to the educators, often with the guards, that they have different moments from us, that they gather them as night falls. But still that day I found myself on the last bench before the world with Almarina huddled in surprise.

I would've wanted to say: 'Those are some nice tiles.' I really would've wanted to say that but I couldn't any more; she had given me something enormous and I had to thank her.

'I had an abortion too, I was eighteen, I'd just started university. It's horrible, but I got my period back after forty days.'

I told her the truth but I would've lied to her too, I would've said it even if it had been a lie. I was trying to say that it gets better, that it doesn't only happen to rape victims, that she and I were similar in many respects.

And as I was trying to make her feel that, I felt it.

'And you're happy you got it back?'

'I am.'

'Do you think you'll want a child of your own one day?'

'I don't know, I always wanted to be a doctor or work in a perfume shop.'

'A perfume shop?'

'Making perfumes, taking these plants, see? And putting them in alcohol, pure alcohol, the one you use with spirits, you put the leaves or flowers in it and you get perfume. You can make it with oils too, but oils cost more.'

We spent a fair amount of time picking flowers without moving, we set up a large biological plant in a land that could've been, from what we said, either Lucania or Romania. We flattened where needed, then with our white coats and hairnets, we stepped into a lab and drop by drop, we chose the vials of essence for our production. Every now and then she'd point to the wall with the sentry boxes and the barbed wire, because all we could see there by now was the blinking neon sign of the perfume shop: ALMARINA.

It's almost Christmas in Nisida, and things are about to happen. Several kids will be out on special licence, Christmas Day lunch, Christmas Eve dinner, and two or three will come back with small doses of coke shoved up their arses. The director will order a cell search. Maybe they'll find something, maybe they won't, and if they do they'll start a thorough investigation so that no one innocent gets dragged into it, they were just in the same place at the same time. Which means school won't start again on the 7th of January like everywhere else, but whenever we'll be able to, in small pieces: a square root will be assigned to someone in another wing, maybe that kid who doesn't give a toss about maths and looks at me through lowered eyes, a hint of a smile. Who knows where they learn sarcasm so early, how to use all the muscles in their faces, minuscule tendons drawing contempt and mockery. Who knows how they're able to paint that inscrutable sentiment onto their faces, when even Dürer needed to look at his reflection to learn his own portrait. And my inmates can't own mirrors.

I hate them. I hate them because I'm three times their age and I shouldn't hate them.

I hate them because if they know contempt this early it means they were targeted with contempt too early, and I should understand them and know how to welcome them, and change vice into virtue or my role as an educator is void, or I might as well ask to be transferred to another school. And because I feel all of this and I can't do any of this, I hate them.

Hatred is a well sparing no one, so down I go along the slimy rope, no matter how hard I grasp at it, and sure, I don't reach the bottom but I see glimmering among the snakes: there's an IV drip in my right arm, something went wrong during the abortion procedure, i never saw him again. an old woman in my grandmother's resting home is yelling at me because i'm playing cards wrong. i'm asking a french person for help in italian, in english, i'm fainting, *s'il vous plait* i say and she flails her hands and shakes her head, as i fall to ground i understand her: she's telling me she doesn't understand me. blurry shapes all male, all the same, tell me that the reason i'm arguing with them like that is because of my period, or it's just about to arrive. the gynaecologist tells me that if i'm not getting pregnant it's because of that abortion twenty years ago: i believe him. a man wearing brown under the neon light, just outside the morgue, just after seeing what used to be my husband on the butcher's block, tells me 'so how about a nice funeral?' Emilia steals a chocolate coin from Ilenia and she says it's my fault: the teacher believes her. the gynaecologist tells me that if i'm not getting pregnant it is because i'm too stressed from work: my husband believes him.

And so you, rejecting square roots with your sarcastic smile, you grab on to the rope with one hand and reach to me with the other to help me back up:

'Now's not the time for maths, I gotta write a letter, it's gotta get there before Christmas: can you help me?'

I pour my entire weight into your grasp, and with all the strength of your seventeen-year-old body you pull me out of the well and back into the classroom.

I don't know how to write a letter. I know how to present an elegant theorem demonstration, compile a thesis, maybe a scientific article, or set a budget.

'For a year after I graduated, I did the books for a shop near home, where I'd like them to hire Almarina.'

My colleagues laugh, plaid blankets on their laps in the staffroom while, beyond the bars, cruise ships slowly sail by.

'Does he need to write a love letter?'

'What was your dissertation about?'

'Start from an epistolary collection you like, Jacopo Ortis or something, those were about love, right Aurò?'

But Aurora shifts the weight elsewhere.

'You're obsessed with Almarina.'

'She needs somewhere to go after she gets out of here.'

'The director will send her to don Valentino, you'll see.'

I don't like the director. I can't say anything against him, he's never been rude or lacking in anything, but I don't like him. It's the smile that doesn't convince me: how can a youth detention centre director be smiling, and how can he accept what he is. He's holding kids where they don't want to be, deciding their daily schedules, being the window between childhood and labels, and this window has to be made of iron and rules and strict timings to adhere to while waiting for visits and solitude. That's why I don't like the director: he's the director of a youth detention centre and I can't get out of my head that it's more natural to join the navy or become a cleaner than to be appointed as a prison director.

Inside, this place is wonderful – and out there is the city that forces you to all or nothing, a cumbersome life, a violated family, war, bombings you're fleeing from, the old guy who sends you to steal and the one who knocks you up, the boyfriend who steals his dad's gun, the mother who didn't see, the one who saw too much, the one who wasn't able to say. Out there you're a beggar in the world. Out there are the children tossed away like a litter of kittens, and kids who shoot up on the tracks of the *circumvesuviana* just before the 11 a.m. express; and the woman in her nightgown sitting on the tobacconist's stool with her eyes glued to the lottery screens. Inside, this place is wonderful, it's everything that our kids have never had, starting with him, the director. There he is and he seems ingratiatory to me but he's the height of responsibleness to them, shouldering mistakes like Christ on the cross. He opens doors as much as he can, mornings here are busy with social workers and volunteers, it's all meetings, and basketball teachers and football teachers and the choir teacher makes passes at me and Pierluigi, who has chosen to spend the rest of his life giving shape to pottery vases. I know. I've never even seen a truncheon used in here. I have seen guards end up in hospital, I've seen a flying chair one day pierce a guard through the back of his neck, and not even then was any violence shown to the kids. But prejudice predates reality too much. There's no time left to have pure eyes, for them to make their own minds up; accepting a change of opinion means disappearing. The most we can do, in these sealed compartments we live in, is to crack them open a little, keeping them ajar to hear the other. And confirm that yes, it is different.

The director is different and I don't trust him, I want nothing to do with him, with the borders of his role that edge into politics, with the look he casts upon his own children as he leaves at night, while knowing that these other kids are still in here. I didn't like a talk he gave me about becoming grown ups so fast.

'Grown ups like you,' I had to tell him, because his degree of proximity with crime is higher than mine.

Nonetheless, I am seeing this man tomorrow.

I start with an epistolary text I like, the only one I find at home without looking too hard, part of a series that

Antonio moved into a box. I think that's how our marriage began: we mixed books. The books on rational mechanics stopped being by themselves to one side, there where they had found some space, wary, ready to set off again in case it didn't work out, and they all went to live together. (Our first dinners were all like that, trying to meet up in the past: 'When you did *Analysis 2* with Mittone, his assistant was Gallo, and three years later my exam was with Gallo.') Two different editions of the same book got mixed up, and school classics met, as did two long-lost brothers of an edition of *Berkeley Physics Course*. Sections were invented: 'local history', 'politics', 'poetry', the labels only existing in our minds and now that he's dead only in mine, because death has this element of despair – you are left as the sole witness of something, of invisible wealth, of spectacular days.

I start with an epistolary text I like, with an orange cover that attracts the boys in class: today I head straight for Ciro and leave it on his desk.

'In here there's a bit of everything: letters to children, mum, wife, siblings and friends, what do you need?'

Ciro had already forgotten, he's inconsistent, he really just needs the latest style of shoes, that's what he'll tell his mother, no hint of punctuation. But then he'll write a letter to his wife: they got married as soon as he was sentenced and during a period of leave they had a baby.

'What did Gramsci do?'

'What does it matter? Do I ask you what you did? He was in prison, and these are his prison letters. They'd give him a sheet of paper every fortnight and he had to make it last, but you can write a whole notebook if you want, huh, and Miss Aurora will even check it for you.'

I can't tell him Gramsci hadn't done anything because I can't risk insulting them if they've been thieves and killers and accomplices, and everyone has to start to make themselves anew, and we only have this time and this ship on which to set the sails and hope to make headway: 'I have become convinced that even when everything is or seems lost, one must quietly go back to work, starting again from the beginning [. . .] I don't want to be either a martyr or a hero.'

Ciro calls me something different every day. To him I'm teach, miss, professor, but also 'can you believe this one' and *this one* is me and he says so in front of me, because what can I do to him? A student in a school would get a warning, a time out, a visit to the principal.

But here the classroom without bars is their only opportunity, and they can't be thrown out, and when they get out for real they'll set off fireworks in the yards behind their homes, filled with washed clothes and wicker chairs and mod scooters. They'll buy them from the Chinese shops in Gianturco without even checking the price. And our principal is off-site, in the Provincial Centre for Adult Education in corso Malta, on the other side of the city, which is like crossing an entire continent; and that principal is beyond just roads and people and buildings and churches, a distance which becomes time only an astrophysicist can calculate. And what does a warning mean to a boy who saw his name on a piece of paper with a sentence underneath?

Ciro opens the book at a random page, then closes it again and pushes it away. Almarina then asks me if she can keep it, gets up and takes the long way round, the route that kids take when they're worried you might say no, or that they shouldn't have asked at all. It's just a book, and I'm sure I can leave it with her, even though it came in with me and used to be Antonio's. Death is also an opportunity no longer to have to ask for permission.

The third time she can't solve the inequality I lose my patience, and I never lose my patience.

I heard her one afternoon with her classmates mocking me with 'aaah, was it that hard?' And they all laughed those small mirthless laughs they have left in their throats.

But it's easy: I head back to the paper.

'The sharp point is towards the smaller number, OK?'

'Yes.'

'So, for example, 8 is smaller than 9 and I write it like this, right? Because the point goes towards the smaller number . . . Now, if I place the 9 first and the 8 after, how do I write the symbol?'

Almarina is red in the face, she's sweating, she's terrified of making a mistake and she stops. So I also need to stop.

The moment I stop I place my feet back on the cold prison tiles and I look outside, towards the willows, and I realise.

'It's OK, I'm sorry,' I tell her. 'All of you, I'm sorry.'

I call the guard, leave them all inside and I go to look for Aurora in the yard, as she's walking with the captain.

'Did you leave them alone?' she asks me as soon as she sees me.

'No, the guard is there.'

Without saying anything we look at the time: for a second we're all in the same fraction of the world, in which there are still twenty minutes to the end of my lesson.

'I left them to solve an equation,' I say. 'I'll head back now.' But it's not true and I go red in the face, and I head up the stairs and sweat, caught in the mistake I couldn't avoid, just like Almarina just then.

'Hey, teacher,' the captain calls me from below, his gorgeous eyes looking at me. 'She's also going soft on you.'

'What do you mean?'

And this is what I realised, which is different from understanding. Understanding is born deep, changes design, shifts and lands. Realisation hits us like an arrow does a target, and afterwards you just have to hope that it's the same for everyone, or forget about it forever.

It happened to Newton, to Copernicus, to Galileo, to me, teacher of class A029, newly qualified in 1999, fully qualified in 2005, as I won't turn on the heating tonight because the ceiling is too high and I'd be wasting heat.

Wrapped in darkness and bed sheets, I can only hope that what the captain told me is true, or forget about it forever: because I want Almarina to study and know and learn and catch up and get good, and do better than her classmates, and be the best of my students, and graduate and find a good job (which reminds me I need to check at the perfume shop if they need anyone). A good job as a shop assistant, so we need to sniff out the brains and she has to train for that job.

'*Need to. Has to.* She'll do what she can, we'll do what we can,' Aurora replies, after dark but she still answers. I can see them, my friends looking at their phones and excusing themselves: 'I have to take this, it's her.' And all the others on that side, the relatives, everyone just nodding in the way that means both 'poor thing' to me and 'poor thing' to them.

That's how I fall asleep, sitting cross-legged on the bed, shrouded in my blanket and shoulders to the wall, phone in my hand, because the alarm is set for 6.35 every morning, just those extra five minutes to have a small breakdown before getting up.

And as soon as I fall asleep, I dream of having big loop earrings piercing my lobes.

Those of you who judge are likely to believe in love at first sight, but other forms of sudden love make you suspicious. Friendships are suspicious, love for one's students has patronising echoes, and deep respect for the elderly seems to be a cover for who knows what element lacking in our past. You want love to proceed by steps, you want to see a linear path, morbidly watching everything. But no, you can't watch: the heart is opaline and checking your conscience is for the unhappy.

That's how I connected with Almarina, as we were watching the sea and I was telling her how my husband was a wonderful swimmer. How he'd disappear for hours behind the last strip of land that I could see from the beach, and I'd lie down a bit, read a bit, feeling a little betrayed and eventually terrified. And when he'd come back and nothing had happened and all of reality was still the same and it was actually really quite beautiful – the only thought was which restaurant to pick – I always felt strange that he hadn't melted or dissolved, nor would he be breathing heavily.

'I can't swim,' she told me, there and then.

'You can still learn, even as an adult,' I replied.

That answer didn't just mean what I said, it also meant I would teach her to swim.

Walking into the director's office is an incredible effort. I'd rather it was the evening, I'd rather be drinking in a bar, so I could deal with it. But I'd never invite the director for a drink. Once the choir teacher invited me to the San Carlo opera theatre, but it was *The Merry Widow*, he hadn't even considered it and I had been unable to laugh about it, and everyone was convinced he was keen on me though maybe he just had an extra ticket and didn't want to go alone. The point is that I would never invite the choir teacher to a bar but I'd go to see *The Merry Widow* with the captain. Except that the captain is married and would never invite me, and I would invite him out for a drink but I never will.

When you're a couple there is the opportunity to betray one another, to exact revenge over a small abandonment with guilty interest, coming home and heading straight into the shower, asking yourself if that anxiety in the pit of your stomach is guilt or fear of being found out. All this ends up with the darkness of death as it was utterly irrelevant. Then one day you rise from the pyre you'd lain upon with your husband and, as the flames that should have turned you to ash die, you find yourself not ash but still a body. You touch your forearms, your toes, you look for yourself in the mirror: you still have a nose, even cheekbones to dab a little with blusher to avoid looking drained.

And you can no longer betray anyone.

One thing always happens, something you never thought possible: you start valuing things more, things like marriage, living together, committed relationships. You keep checking the ring finger of everyone your age, women or men.

I took my two wedding rings to the shop where we'd bought them. We spent so much time at the large table taking our measurements, choosing the designs, the font for the names and date. ANTONIO. ELISABETTA.

We danced afterwards. In the living room, a Shostakovich waltz that he'd bought from the newsagent's and that he always put on when it was his turn to clean the house. The CD was already in the player and Antonio invited me to dance. I was becoming aware as I danced, hitting the table, leaning my forehead against his shoulder to avoid dizziness, I was realising, shuffling through the kitchen door, that my husband was a beautiful man, tall, wide shoulders that bring so much substance, that the house was full, illness wouldn't have scared us, boredom would be a bearable accident. It was a waltz, its heart in a major key, so I didn't listen to the opening theme: I didn't notice death following us as we twirled. It was Shostakovich's second waltz and I can no longer listen to it.

When nine years later I headed back to the same table, the goldsmith couldn't possibly remember me, but to me it was as if I'd just said goodbye to him that morning. I reached out my hand, and so did he, thinking I wanted to shake but instead I loosened my fist and poured the two rings and my own surprise into his palm. Thinking about it now I realise the gesture could have been seen in different ways: was I selling some gold? Was I asking for an appraisal?

So it must have been my face.

It must have been the ash from the pyre that covered the table, because he said: 'My condolences,' and I said 'Thank you,' and he said 'Do you want me to make some earrings out of them? You'd get some nice thick loops.'

I said yes.

I was thankful: people who trade in my city assign things the value they have, they watch over the ritual and understand those standing before them better than they do themselves. They come up with formulae to protract death and life which would otherwise mean nothing.

But my ears aren't pierced, never have been. I have a memory like a childhood night-light featuring my grandmother's insistence and my mother speaking of tribal rites and myself secretly hoping for my grandmother to win but knowing my mother would instead. I never got them pierced but I said yes to the goldsmith: yes, let's make two nice loops, in that way in which sometimes you live with and recognise someone else. But someone normal, common, an everyday someone, someone you don't know. We don't always need to play the hero, even if sometimes we can be one for real. And so I said yes because if that was the most natural suggestion the goldsmith could come up with then it had to be right.

It's a vaguely sweet feeling, the one you get when you adhere to the image that others have of you: like pain fading as the medicine kicks in. You yield, little by little, to being a little less than who you are. Life already gives us too many opportunities to feel different and alone, after all.

Inside the morgue, in front of the sterile metal table, my husband covered with a sheet, the pressure of my in-laws behind me, I crossed myself. I often think about it in burning shame, because neither myself nor Antonio was Catholic. And the only answer I can give myself is this: I didn't know what to do. You left me alone to deal with your death, you piece of shit, alone, and all I could do was what most people do when they're dealing with mourning. I am neither a martyr nor a hero.

'I got the file for Luchian Almarina. Is that right?'

The director has a large wedding ring, very tacky, and these long fingers; his entire appearance is one of evasion. When I think about him I remember almost through him.

'I imagine you're going to ask me to speak on her behalf.'

'What happens to this girl when she gets out of here?'

'Did she seduce you? There's always a couple of inmates who seduce us.'

'I don't think she has done anything, she has only been done to.'

'So you're judging. That's not what the State is asking of you, nor of me. We execute. Me, I execute the guardianship judge's orders; you, the ministerial syllabus.'

'Who gives a fuck, excuse me, of what I need to do according to the State. I'm saying that I care about this inmate because she's a victim.'

'And the others aren't? Are you ranking them? Dr Maiorano, do you know how many of your colleagues have come here, over the years, to ask the same thing about this kid or that kid in particular? Miss Aurora has christened an inmate's child. Can you imagine what that means? There was this kid, and another kid in her arms, and we had to keep them in prison.'

'That's the point: I'm not afraid as long as she's in here. I'm afraid of the outside, director, of the city, of Italy. This world scares me, those who beat her almost to death the first time will do it again, and I'm not talking about the father, I'm talking about fathers. Fathers scare me, director, even you.'

'Believe me, mothers aren't that much better. The other day during visits a mother told her son that if he betrayed the family she'd disown him, she told him through gestures but we know all those gestures by now. And who do you think gets cocaine into here? The mothers, so that their kids can use it as currency. The mothers aren't better, Miss Maiorano. We need to look at each case by case, minute by minute. Why do you want to know about Almarina?'

'Because I feel more responsible towards her. It happens? Getting close to a student? Almarina keeps all of the books I bring her, she held on to Gramsci and I felt sorry because if I'd thought about it I would've brought her *Jane Eyre* . . .'

'Can I tell you why you felt sorry? Can I try? I've been thinking about it for twenty years. So. I think you felt sorry because if there's a guilty minor, there's a guilty adult. And it's not enough to dip in and out of taking on the responsibility of guilt.'

'But I don't feel guilty.'

'Responsible, then.'

'Yes, responsible.'

'Why more so with Almarina?'

'Because I feel as though she can make it, and I don't want to make her miss this one opportunity.'

'I always think they can all make it. Even the ones with crap for brains who want, who wish, to be shot dead, those who can't wait to be back on the street. I always think they can all make it.'

'I got close to her. I like her. I remember what went through my mind at sixteen, director, and I know that everything is different except the body. The body is the same, the pimples, the periods, the cold and the heat, feeling well or hungry. I go to bed and I think of Almarina sleeping and I fall asleep. And I wake up at dawn and I think that one day I won't see her any more, just like all the others I never saw again, and I won't sleep any more. And I don't want to die from lack of sleep, director.'

At the top of Almarina's file, in the centre, is a nice laurel wreath. Sometimes on the Rettifilo you see young women leave the university with wreaths like this, and I have one too, hanging in the kitchen. I use it when I cook liver, or a sauté.

Then you move down, through the public prosecutor of the Republic for the youth court; the judge of the preliminary trial for the youth court; the youth court; the public prosecutor for the appeal court; the youth branch of the appeal court; the youth monitoring judge.

Here it turns into Braille, we have to use our fingers to read it, and up we go, eyes closed, the director and I, feeling. ex. art. and ff. c.c.p following appeal, the sentence n. given by, deposited on, concluding trial of proc. n. R.G. with repeal for sentence n. deciding for appeal filed on, declares.

Mountains rise from Almarina's files ending with soft sounds, Postavarul, Peleaga: it's summer, there's work in the fields, our fingers fall into the valley along a riverbed. There's a house, she's eight years old, her mother's belly is enormous, her movements are slow. Inside, the child that will kill her. 'Almarina, help me with the sheets.' But as soon as she throws covers and pillows on the floor, Almarina jumps onto them.

The youth branch of the appeal court sentence her to three months of incarceration. A Maria Lătărețu song rises from Almarina's file:

Şi mi-am pus în gând
Ca să zbor în vânt
Să dau de pământ
Să mor mai curând*

And because the wind in our faces is blowing from Transylvania, to avoid dying of exposure the director and I make the enormous effort of closing the file. He takes the right side, I take the left, pushing against the blizzard until the two pages close back in the centre. We stay there a while, in silence, hands on the cover, until our breathing calms down. And then I remember the reason I booked a meeting with him.

'Can I stay here on Christmas Eve, director?'

'I'll let you know.'

It's easier with adults, everyone says so, and I wouldn't know because I've always taught children and teenagers, so I believe it: it's really difficult with them.

Among the many intelligent women I've seen flee this vessel never to make port again there is a volunteer who used to teach drama. She had worked in so many prisons that she was sure she'd come here and be fine. She had even had a relationship with an ex-inmate, and it was fun hearing her talk about love between inmates and teachers: the other way round, the one you don't picture, from the free person to the incarcerated one.

---

* From the song *Lie Ciocârlie*. 'I have thought about / flying away with the wind / to find land / and die early'

(I've always been in two minds about volunteers as this underlines the difference between classes, or roles, or between lucky and unlucky backgrounds, which is precisely the point where life becomes unacceptable. It's the only possible alternative to doing nothing as everything is going to the dogs, but then: helping at the soup kitchen for Christmas while you have a family at home. eden achieved with weekly four-hour shifts. scheduled suffering. that spike of relief as you slide the key in your front door. leaving a hospital and seeing your own healthy children. reaching for a mastiff who happily licks your hand. Blessed be the country that does not need volunteers.)

This one person, Agata, the drama teacher, was different. She really had fallen in love with her inmate, she'd tell us laughingly, because she had lost a whole family for it: her own. The former inmate had spent a week fucking her and then headed back to his wife, while she hadn't found any version of the story to tell her husband.

We laughed as we listened to her tell us, glass in hand on the sofa at home; even Antonio laughed, despite feeling closer to the betrayed than the inmate. That's how it is with general inmates: none of us is able to identify with them (we seem only to imagine ourselves as political prisoners). In any case, Agata was a funny woman and she was able to joke about a lot of things, except Nisida. She stayed a while, she tried her best, and her best was great, and it was the right way too, and then she never came back. Now she lives in Genoa, we're still in touch and we talked about important things when I became a widow.

But what she told me when she talked about her Nisida defeat was about the limitations of a mother.

She told me that when she visited other prisons, the time dedicated to drama was a moment of complete freedom. The inmates could do anything they wanted, find distraction from their condition, exorcise the pain, hope for a sentence conversion. Drama, like any other workshop, was an alternative to prison. In Nisida, on the other hand, it was an alternative to being a teenager, something they knew very little about. It was an alternative to a real life they had yet even to taste: travelling, sex, hanging out with friends, not listening to their mothers. Inside there we recreated exactly what our own children wanted to emancipate themselves from.

I remembered the pure hatred I felt when my mother prohibited me from going to a party. I saw it crystallise before my eyes and I was right back inside it when Agata told me what wasn't working. And that's when I understood that to the heart of a sixteen-year-old, we are the guards, not the uniformed staff, us, trying to help them give sense to their life, the almost mothers.

'Teach, I'm giving you your book back.'

'So, did you like it?'

'Didn't finish it.'

'Was it too hard?'

'Not the writing, it's just that he has all of these people to write to: the wife, the wife's sister, two kids, even his mum, and then his friend. And they all reply, and so when he writes, he knows that they'll reply sooner or later.'

Almarina's head is no longer shaved, she's letting her hair grow out: as she stands in front of me I see it as it blossoms on her forehead, runs behind her ears, takes shape. And as her hair grows she raises her posture, shoulders straight, and her chest grows too.

'Is there anyone you can write a Christmas letter to?'

'Just you, teach.'

'Your brother?'

'I don't even know if he can read. When I left him. But it was the only way. You understand? His name's Arban.'

'And where is he now?'

'I don't know. For his sake, that's what they said, because sometimes siblings meet again and the good one follows the bad one's example. They said when he's eighteen he can come and find me.'

And it's not that I understand, but rather I'm plunged into an even deeper place, a cave that looms over me and shelters me; it's filled with all the people who save their children, siblings, nieces, nephews, or someone else's children. Arms raised to the sky, women and men offering children so they may be seen and taken, raising a life that's worth more than their own, because there's a ranking in life too: those who know how to love look after it.

'Yo teach, where did you go?'

The kids mock me, they mimic my expression as I watch the sea. So I turn back to the class, and Almarina is different in my eyes.

'Did you know that Madame Bovary bought a lovely set of writing paper even though she had no one to write to?'

'Who's Madame Bovary?'

'Okay, I'll bring you that one too tomorrow, but we need to focus on angles today. Come on class, last lesson before Christmas break, look at your worksheets. What is an angle?'

'The por-tion of a plane con-tained be-tween two rays o-ri-gi-na-ting from the same point.'

'And that means?'

'. . .'

'OK. Look at the hands on the clock . . .'

'Oh, I've got it.'

'What did you get?'

'That it's time to go.'

It is there, this confidence, the sign that I exist. It has taken me three years to build it, and once you've achieved it, it's passed on, it's passed down. The kids leave, for other prisons, for other crimes, or maybe for Edinburgh and a better life, but they all leave a secret code within the Nisida walls – among them there must be a list of who deserves what.

In the early days they never looked me in the eye. And I remember it, those half-voices, lowered heads, smiles among the boys. Being able to tell you without ever telling you that you are no one, they're wasting time with you, and you're wasting yours. What they know about maths is enough, all you need for cocaine is addition and subtraction and no matter what the unit is, all you need is to see where the needle stops. Walking into the classroom as if forced; that is, actually forced. Forced to sit at their desks, the size of animals, if they'd met you outside they wouldn't waste a second on a woman like you so who are you in here? Or maybe another type of contempt, another flavour: you're a teacher and teachers have no destiny, they're people who don't risk their own skin and so they'll get nothing other than a gift from the enemy State thirteen times a year, and be grateful for it.

I'd see Aurora, the hard features of her face, never yielding to anger, to laughter: just like the kids, never raising her voice, never offended, never considering them. Were they, weren't they there, in class, these inmates? How could she, Aurora, explain grammar with a face like stone? Stone carved by a million marks, a wrinkle for every kid, every barrier raised or lowered, outer door open or shut, every brawl, every cell, in there for the last thirty years: drawn all over her face was Nisida.

I didn't like this woman, who without ever changing her tone of voice, with the same voice as when she took the register, would tell us in the staffroom about how many times this one girl had stabbed her sister to death. Just like that. But there was this one thing that made me suspicious: a discordant note that was a like a crack through which I slipped despite myself. Aurora brought a jar of sweets with her to class. Generic boiled sweets with coloured wrappers, like they used to have forty years ago at Sunday school. And she'd leave the jar on the horseshoe of desks during the lesson. On one side of the U there are the boys, on the other the girls, the teacher walks between them so everyone can see everyone else, the guard from behind the glass door keeps an eye, there are no bars on the window, outside is Porto Paone and a few slow sailing boats. And the kids who refused even to look at me, they took of that jar like children. Patricides, matricides, dealers, thieves, a hand slipped into the tight opening when it's their turn, the wrappers between their fingers, the sugar melting in their mouth.

I also had to take of the jar if I wanted to explain trigonometry.

So one day, pointing my index finger to a piece of paper that a Tunisian kid was writing on, too slowly, I can't remember what it was, he raised his face to me and stared me right in the eye.

'I know, I know what I'm supposed to be doing,' he told me, proud, mature, aware, even irritated. What changed my life was that he searched my eyes to tell me, and I saw them: I had been allowed to look.

All his family was inside them, a large family, eight siblings and a mother who did medical jabs for people in their homes; she disinfected the glass syringes by boiling them in a small iron case like a sardine tin. The older brother leaving and sending good news from Germany, and an energy inside that doesn't let you sleep, the certainty of being able to succeed, of being the smartest, the smallest brother who never fell ill. The one who will cross the sea and its borders and one day drive a Mercedes in the streets of Munich. He will send a photo to his mother of himself holding a blonde girl; he'll send it from a smartphone and the photo will fly in the ether and will console the syringe-lady.

I will never forget the eyes of my Tunisian student who had understood the assignment, the dark of his pupils. I sometimes look for it in my memory, when I'm confused, when I can't fully distinguish what's true and what's false. I sieve life through it and what remains in my hands is what truly matters.

'Miss Maiorano, the third table.'

'Thank you.'

'No, the one under the glass, the boy will come to set it up.'

They call it glass but it's a heavy plastic sheet hung up in winter, to stop the wind blowing up from the sea. After two days, it's thick with brine and it fogs up. And so we all stay each at our own table, all singles on our lunch break staring at an off-white plastic sheet, beyond which we might see the shadow of the sea. Some of us say hello. Others, as though in a train carriage, sit facing the opposite way, but still alone, always alone, everyone alone, watching a muted TV set. And so the wave, the clinking of forks, the uncorking of a bottle.

'Am I the first?' someone I'd fucked had asked. I wasn't sure I'd understood. I'm fifty years old, but I had understood: there was this spectre whining about my naked body and yes, he was the first after my mourning, but I didn't feel it was a question that deserved answering, not to him.

So better to sleep alone, to eat alone: the wave, the forks clinking, the humming of the red Coca-Cola fridge.

At eight in the morning the bakery shines, its heat a mirage as I step in. It's nice in here, there is no need to head outside, down into the city, head back home. Francesco is wearing all white, his hair up, his hands warm, and he's telling me how to make panettone, why they're placed upside down, how you put filling inside. I listen, but mostly I'm listening to my body, the strong smell of vanilla, the expectation of nativity that I no longer ever feel. So focused, so attentive, Francesco so far from the street where he stabbed, the hands that wounded now filled with flour, like an angel, or a toga-draped man about to introduce himself to the people in the acropolis of an ancient city. The pastry chef who travels up here around Christmas time is listening with a smile: the boy has learned and he's learned to explain.

'Make eight slices so Dr Maiorano can take it to the others, so they can have breakfast.'

And when Francesco's hand stops to think, I stop him.

'How many cuts to make eight slices? Think.'

'Maro teach, do we have to do maths here too?'

'Maths is already in the panettone, I'm not the one who put it there. Come on.'

'I'm starting to cut it.'

'No, think. If you make a cross, how many slices?'

'Four.'

'So?'

So he sets to work, but there's a smile rising inside him that he tries to hold back but can't.

There isn't just maths in the cake, there are also the two pieces of metal jutting out of the wall holding up the lines of clean washing. Francesco needs to dodge them to enter the basement where he grew up. The TV set is enormous and always on, a woman pushes water and bleach with her broom, hits his feet. 'What did you come back for' is the first thing she says, maybe the only one. Those who might want to peer over the door of the basement would see a man in a vest, smoking, zoned out at the table, and above him, in a small wooden loft, an old woman and a child, asleep. In those places, they must have taught him, with words or with silences, that it's better to be fast with your hands than with your thinking.

But they can't avoid being smart for long and while Francesco acts swiftly and surely with the cut, certain that it'll be eight slices, he can't help being proud of himself.

The pastry chef potters around here and there but he's also smiling because he can recognise the fire: with caution, careful not to be seen, on the same wave of complicity we catch each other's gaze for a second.

That's how the director finds me, my face in white chocolate.

'Miss, I need to speak to you about that thing. So, to make things easier I would forward a request to Luchian Almarina's judge to do the opposite: that is to say, you pick her up from midday on Christmas Eve to 7 p.m. on Boxing Day. What do you say? The girl can have her permit for Christmas, no problem, she just needs a permanent address . . .'

'All to make things easier for him. He's selfish. We all knew he was selfish.'

Aurora brings me a drink.

In this neighbourhood, it's all parallel roads meeting at right angles as if it were Manhattan. From east to west, the roads take you to the sea, from south to north they lead from the chimneys to Sybil's cave. Short roads, a short neighbourhood posing as levy to the city, its perspective, its shame, its nightmare, its hope. The low cubic houses were the ones for the workers, low because they'd never get lifts installed. Bagnoli knows everything, has seen everything, before and after, from a different corner of the city: it has seen fascists building their Liberty-style second houses, has seen the first blast furnace rise like a bell tower; then it saw a column of smoke dull the sea, tar the seagulls; then it saw the column of its women and its men heading to labour at the steelworks day and night. It saw the factory being closed, the Chinese arriving to take it apart piece by large piece and move it away across the water, it saw cancer grasp onto the lungs of those who worked inside, the return of the beaches, the workers turned lifeguards, the lidos becoming autonomous social centres; is the metro coming or not, is the cleaner coming or not, men in white panama hats talking sense, fat women in black leggings getting inked, someone eating and throwing paper on to the ground, someone else organising a beach clean up. City of science comes by here, the pride parade comes by here, every minister comes by here, every head of state, every wealthy person but only the truly wealthy, the Camorra comes by here dreaming of buying up everything, the beach, the people and Nisida. Nisida to make it into a resort, taking it away from those who clean up from their small crimes like dealing cocaine and giving it to those who commit big crimes such as importing it and selling it, taking the place away from the possibility of the spirit to give it to the certainty of money, and finally to let yachts moor here.

Aurora crosses the road with the beer glasses in her hands, as we do here, in this neighbourhood where women have freed themselves from the yoke of the home through the yoke of the factory; and now they work at supermarket tills and when their shift ends they're all here, having a drink before heading home, with friends, with colleagues, the pharmacist and the custodial staff, as if it were Oslo, as if it were Soho, a club of single women, with a glass in hand, at the centre of the park; but it's better than Soho because the sun here warms you up even in December, and no one cares if you leave home in your slippers.

'Don't you feel up to it?' asks Aurora from under her foam moustache.

'It's not that I don't feel up to it ... it just feels inappropriate.'

'You don't feel up to it. You're scared.'

'Those seventy-two hours will never be over, dammit.'

'That's the same for everyone, when it comes to Christmas.'

'Dammit, Aurora. How do you think it'll go?'

'Only the Sibyl knows.'

And three beers in I'm already in the cave, waiting for a response written on a palm leaf.

'Sometimes, when I'm on the night shift, especially in summer, I feel a massive weight on my shoulder. As though the sky has actually got heavier, and you know what it is?'

The captain strikes with his sickle on to the scarp, the kids are all on the same road that plunges into the sea. Some further up, some further down, they're all at work, hoods down to their eyes. Everyone focusing on one spot on the path. Fighting whatever they can fight: weeds, asphodels mostly, taking advantage of the mild winter and the fifteen degrees of this sunlit morning.

'It's the weight of the entire world from which I'm trying to protect them. I scare myself, I scare myself so much that sooner or later, someone will come to power and they'll do it: they'll send us away from here to make a hotel out of it. That sooner or later they'll replace the director and in here everything will fade into the other places I've worked at, places with no way out.'

'This one any good, sir? Looks like rosemary.'

The kid brings us a couple of sprigs and we smell them, rubbing them between our fingers.

'This is lavender, leave it in.'

The kid walks away again, holding a weapon. Now that I've thought about it I look for them among the bushes and I see them all with their shining weapons: they could gut us or gut each other or start fighting each other. They've already done just that, far from here.

'Without this scarp and the lavender and all this, I can't help them. Even you, without the books, without maths, you can't help them.'

The captain looks to the open sea and protects Nisida from incursions. There, away from here, on land, is a world where all the blades become weapons. Beyond the jetty, beyond lido Pola, where the road splits between the steelworks and the Seiano cave; inside the fierce dynamics of the neighbourhoods, inside the road with its stone secrets, inside the cars of six or seven people, inside the cocaine molecule (four asymmetrical carbon atoms). Fat adults, judgemental and thieving, overflow from scooters, use one leg as a pivot to turn round and zoom back the wrong way, showing their gun, and all it means is 'let me make this clear.' It's in the via Foria at 6.30 p.m. on a day like any other that a blade is used to slash another kid's jugular. Not here where the scarp needs weeding, and then later where all will need piling into a small fire away from the wind, after wetting the ground in a circle around it.

Going back to the cells come evening, feeling the warm water cleaning the skin and the smell of soil rising with the soap. (Faces are tanned and the shoes that fitted but three months ago are starting to feel tight: that must be why you can't wait to run down to the dining area to devour everything.)

Among the rows of strawberry grapes, they play children's games: throwing soil at each other.

'Are your sisters-in-law happy you have guests for Christmas?'

'No.'

The captain smiles at me and the sky clears. If this were a normal life we'd be heading for the tableland, inside the extinct volcano rim, where the water shines, and I'd let myself be held tight and I'd make love to him. I think of this poor body of mine and I feel pity for it as I would for a stranger: who holds you at the age of fifty, really holds you, if you don't have a partner? But no life is normal and the sea in Nisida is just an illusion, and the captain is already heading back up the path to save a mole from the dog's paws.

They tower over me. They're men with wide shoulders, you can see the muscles shifting under their T-shirts. During the lesson, each of them appears like a giant, then they sit at their desks, crouching into a position they haven't really thought about, that they can't hold, they're immediately restless. They're there as a favour to me and I want to kiss them on the forehead, if only they'd let me do so, if I only wouldn't immediately become stupid. If the guards out there weren't always watching our movements through the glass. The guards watch and the kids adhere to their gaze, and so do I.

We are as we are seen.

They have more swagger, I'm stricter and more aloof. We keep to our point, as the smallest of points ourselves, and everything else remains outside. We need to leave this smallness, this moment, we need to make do with what we have. For the last lesson before the holidays, I'm doing the taxonomy of living species.

We're working on *Homo sapiens*; as I'm writing on the board there are messages being exchanged between desks. KINGDOM – ANIMALIA. Lives which are just this and sixteen more years ahead, in another generic prison. We've seen what they can become, in a prison that isn't Nisida. And as much as I can chalk PHYLUM – CHORDATA on to the board, all it does is reveal the truth that the lesson is being suspended: prison is a pain that never ends, from which there is no distraction. Everyone who crosses the threshold of a prison knows (and if they don't know, they can feel it) that they're stepping into another place that contradicts what we've been told since childhood: life would not be scary, and we'd never be alone. Prison is precisely that: fear and loneliness. You go to sleep in prison and you wake up in prison. You learn soon enough that the less you do, the better.

What remains with the inmates, after years of low ceilings and shit overflowing from the toilets, are vague flashes of a body they once inhabited. That they used to commit crimes or murders, or they were the only things they could be: small-time dealers, pickpockets, skilled thieves at the piazza Cavour station. That body which supported them, filled with adrenaline, jumping from balcony to balcony, while above them the police helicopters circled in. Or the one that figured out which alley the *falchi* would appear from, and evaded them.

The body that launched itself is now still and quiet. It's the cage that makes these men closer not to animals (because animals is what we are) CLASS – MAMMALIA, but closer to what man wants animals to be.

Because of this enslavement, this underworld so obvious to those walking through the gate, we should have an understanding of the inmates. Just as we understand their victims on the outside. ORDER – PRIMATES. FAMILY – HOMINIDAE. SPECIES – HOMO SAPIENS.

I turn around.

Kadija is taking notes: 'Miss, with an aitch?'

'Yes, *homo*, it's Latin.'

'And for girls?'

'It's the same. Let me explain, take Carlo: on this level Carlo is like a frog. You're laughing but it's true. Then here, Carlo is a goat. Yes, goats give birth to living kids and feed them, so . . . and here he's a chimpanzee, see? They already look closer . . . yes, good, stand up so we can see better, come to the board. Here you are, at this stage you're a creature standing straight, I mean, almost straight, yeah okay, acting with reason, I guess, almost with reason, and expressing himself through language, when you feel like it . . .'

'Teach, who's he like at this stage?'

(Here he's similar to the judge who sentenced him and to his cellmate, to Pythagoras, to the man he strangled in his bed and the one in his speedboat over there, to the girl he fancies and to Leonardo da Vinci, and to the old man with one arm sitting in piazza Nicola Amore who scraped through the remains of a box of pasta.)

'Here he's like me.'

Almarina comes to my car with a bag: she's left nothing in her cell. I'm worried she might have misunderstood, that she didn't realise we're coming back here on Boxing Day evening.

'Did you leave nothing behind because you're worried they'll take your stuff?'

'No, I didn't leave anything because I don't have anything.'

And because the bag of nothing is resting on the back seat, for the first time I see that my car is a nice car, tomato-sauce red with heated seats, and I remember that I keep it in the garage because of it being a nice car. And because Almarina wears worn-out canvas shoes even in December, I look at my feet and I see for the first time that my shoes are nice shoes, even if they're a year old, comfy enough to drive and they give the foot a nice shape. As I cross the jetty, a new feeling rises inside me about my minor luxuries, and along the tuff shore up towards Posillipo the feeling reveals itself for what it is. It suddenly reveals itself in piazza San Luigi, because I have a lipstick in the glove compartment and we both put some on using the rear-view mirror: I'm proud of myself.

I take her to a café, everyone looks at her, looks at us, I am her guardian in the eyes of the world; not because I am committed to bringing her back to prison in seventy-two hours, but rather because I ensure she is waited on hand and foot while we sit at the table, we'll have two small *cassate*, waiter, and two nice coffees. Because the gold of Naples is waiting to stun us into its Christmas trappings. Almarina and I celebrate in the decadent and luxurious way we do here: we go all out, we eat, we drink, we spend money without regrets, because the line is made of infinite points and this point is where we are.

Christmas, for Antonio and I, had become a terrible disappointment: it was always the time when the TV would show toy adverts and all the talk was about children, aimed at children, and you'd have to go to San Gregorio Armeno to pick up small Baby Jesuses to be born in papier-mâché mangers, placed under a piece of batting.

Those with children would set them to decorate the tree and those without showed off round bellies, or maybe I was the one to see all this and just this because even IV treatments had failed and my husband had had enough, he wouldn't wank into another vial, and after however many days stunned on the sofa, doing nothing, he'd come to my rescue with a suggestion: 'We could adopt. There shouldn't be any issues with us.'

I had poured all my sense of purpose and direction into that conditional, and, feverish with change, I had moved from one place to another, I'd slowly taken up its shape, I'd set up the coming days.

We'd researched how to make children: with doctors first, then with lawyers. We'd researched on the Internet, in books, met up with others: travellers along the same path, some further ahead, some luckier, some less lucky, some even further behind, because then we found out (and no one will ever tell you, which means it's like finding a trap on the route, which you either fall into or disarm) that our single attempt at IV fertilisation had brought us straight before the first judge.

It's twelve days in total; each time you end one you're one step higher, a little safer, but the top is still narrower than the base and very few make it all the way up. We'd look at those preceding us to gather strength, like on a final bicycle sprint, yes; but we'd only really understand each other among peers. We'd become friends only with couples our same age, our same background, our same income. The judge would ask us difficult questions with no real answers. Even they wouldn't have had an answer.

Judges sometimes only ask in order to create reality: our answer may be the world's first day.

Or maybe they ask and torture us because they know that the children we're adopting come from such deep despair that even if they were only one day old they would have already internalised it.

Or maybe they ask and torture and watch us leave in tears because that's the fastest way to grow. The fastest way to grow hard, to grow awareness, ready from the start.

And yet there are two places and two sides of the world in this room: on one side there are those of you judging and on the other us, and our nights. And it's not true that we're all equal human beings because equality is not an innate condition, it's something that's built between parties when they look at each other from opposite sides of a table.

We the undersigned spouse surname name, both residing in the city of, married on and cohabiting since, advised that the information within, request according to and to the effect the adoption of one or more minors [of colour] [abused] [at judicial risk] [HIV positive]. Living conditions to follow [in urban centre with access to green spaces]. Availability to adopt a minor with disability: [none] [physical or minor or reversible mental] [only severe physical] [only severe mental] [severe mental and/or physical].

Couples may only indicate one preference.

*

One preference, Antonio. With me turning you onto your side, at night, when you start snoring. With you letting bills go unpaid. With me pretending not to see it but ready to bring it up as soon as you mess up. With you pretending to convince yourself but actually just letting me have this one. With us envying the kids heading down to the beach after 3 p.m.

Let me be clear, your honours: one decides and the other follows suit. One knows and the other will never know, even if it's written down, and one is taking responsibility and the other handing it over. Even though you speak of a couple, your honours, there is no couple: there are separate individuals who would never have wanted to know which box to tick because there is no preference but only the vastness of chance above us, and everything we will have ticked will turn out to be wrong if we'll be unhappy, and right if we'll be happy.

These are papers to which we initially respond no and end up saying yes to everything.

Because one night you wake up and understand that those choices aren't there for you, and that it's not your fate: the questions are the result of years of compassionate systematic naming. They're the tucking in of sheets in orphanages, smiles at newborns in their cribs, open arms waiting to be the finishing line of an uncertain race. And so you see them, through the paper, you enter the vegetable fibre and they're already in there. They have been born, they're grown and they're young, abandoned by parents who are alive or dead, they have arms, eyes, reason, or they don't. If you don't want to you don't see them, but if you do you see them immediately; those boxes don't belong to you, they're definitely not waiting for your pen, those are spaces for the children and the children already exist. You place the tick on the hardest of choices only when you suddenly realise that it's not the parents who make the children, but children who make their parents.

The last judge to meet us is kind; he's sitting against the light so I'll never really remember him. I do remember his silhouette emerging from the desk. He takes minutes of what we say himself, on his computer. As we wait for him in his room, there are children's drawings on the coffee table. (Were they there to keep them busy or to study their hearts?) Because judges have a room, and in that room are sofas and a coffee table, almost like a tiny lounge. In this room there are windows and on some days they open on to the city and its life, and on others the sky is low and they open on to a slate of ice, and it will take thousands of years until mammoth fossils emerge from it.

The judge takes minutes of what we say and we look at the door at the back, as if our son might appear at any moment. I've always imagined him to be a boy, I don't know about Antonio, because we always talk differently from what we dream about, but I dreamt of a boy. And that morning at dawn I received a message from another adoptive mother: it read that there was a child ready. Scoops among us parents, certain bits of news or gossip, coming to our ears, whispered in code.

So I keep looking at the judge against the light a little and at the door a lot and I resist. And for the first time in a line of twelve identical ones, everything seems reassuring.

The judge has read everything we've said, as have other judges like him, in the one hundred and ten days preceding this one; he has held papers that turned into words written by others that turned into things that we said, that turned into the furthest of our thoughts. The judge washes his hands, then he steps into the room and he sees us. He sees a man and a woman (and behind the divide is a child). They're three strangers, they're not related, a few years ago they didn't even know one another. They're in this room because of chance, one of those opportunities and combinations whose number is so vast that it appears infinite. (Behind the divide is a child. No matter what, under any sign and for any reason, if that child is there it means they don't have a home.) In any way, under any sign and for any reason, if those adults are there it's because they're looking. They affirm their lives in the search for a different term to adhere to. Everything is moot between them: once actions are over, words start again, as does the opinion that each has of the other. The truth, which does not exist as an absolute, has the opportunity to arrange itself in this room around this table, and it will be their creation.

But that day the judge greets us like any other day and we realise that the child behind the divide will not be our child and we'll head out for a beer with the rest of the group of parents, like on any other day.

I'm sure it hasn't happened to just me, to become a widow and forget everything: others will have separated, wars will have broken out, others will have fallen ill and died. And these unexpected files, filled with wrong answers, open-ended statements, sentences left without a full stop, they all head to the pulping mills of memory. During the pulping process, they get selected. The value of the memory increases the more defined the selection is: the memory runs along a conveyor belt, frame by frame, hope by hope; impurities and waste are removed from the pulp. At this point in the cycle, the memory contained within the waste paper has gone back to being raw material ready to be worked again, ready to be reformulated. When I met my dead husband, there on the awful morgue table, the second thing I realised was that it would be harder to win an adoption case. My country is like that.

It wasn't until the end of the pulping process that I realised the first thing: that my husband truly was ready to become father to any child who might have come our way, because he was a real man, one guided only by freedom and love, and whoever is ready for that is also ready to die and everything else.

Then there are the immortals, who would never think about this sort of thing.

'Are you alright? Do you need anything? Can I . . .?'

I had forgotten about the bathroom door scenario: since I started living alone, I've always left it open, with layers of bras hanging off the handle by their straps, divided into those still to wear and those to put in the wash.

'Can I?'

Almarina hasn't locked herself in because she's also forgotten what keys are for – when someone stands on the right side, the person who opens or locks – so I walk in and find her sitting on the side of the bathtub, fully clothed, looking at all the products she has found. With the same intensity be it the washing powder or the dispenser for an unbranded soap, the bottle of bleach or the bottle of the only perfume I've used since my teenage years. She looks at them with surprise and awe, and the more coloured the plastic, the more outrageous the colours, the more her eyes sparkle. To own something that can end and needs replacing, I'll realise a few hours later, is so much wealth to her. I'll realise it in the kitchen, and in front of the wardrobe: the metals, the fabrics, the noble materials, the glass, they don't bring her the same joy. She has a dress, and Nisida's kitchen is stocked with shiny steel utensils: it's the empties that excite her.

Her, these days: she starts, sometimes, if someone sets off firecrackers outside, preparing for New Year's Eve; she likes the house; she has difficulty crossing the road; she learns that there's no one on the other side of the cash machine; she learns that the cash machine doesn't give out money freely if you guess the combination, but you're taking it out of your pay; she never cries; she hates the market and loves the supermarket; she sleeps often and without a real schedule; she loves walking through the metro turnstiles with a valid ticket; she wanted to go to Mass on the 25th; the morning of the 26th, Boxing Day, when all the shops are closed, she had a panic attack.

Me, these days: I've turned on the heating, turned it up so high we can grow orchids in the house; I read *Anna, soror* . . . about ten pages every evening; I made *struffoli* according to one of my mother's recipes written by her tidy, round hand and I cried; I had to stay inside the church during Mass because I couldn't lose sight of Almarina, and the congregation rose and fell on the pews like pistons; the morning of the 26th, Boxing Day, when all shops are closed, I had a panic attack.

Us, these days: we painted each other's fingernails; we ate two kilos of sautéed seafood; we watched *Pocketful of Miracles* on the sofa, sitting zigzagged against the back cushion, knees folded and feet meeting in the middle, and when Bette Davis came out in full costume and make-up, we were Bette Davis. On Boxing Day morning, when we had a panic attack, we noticed that the only shop open when all the others are closed is a chemist's. So we went in, and as she squeezed my hand tight and I squeezed my lips tight, I got my ears pierced.

On the 24th of December, a few minutes before midnight, Almarina was asleep. I sat next to her to decide whether or not to wake her (I had to remove the batting covering Baby Jesus in the nativity scene) and I saw she was dreaming. Behind her eyelids, her pupils were moving at the speed of REM sleep, the speed of a passing train, chaotic, over the sleepers. A crowd of old people and young people with gorgeous eyes and women like me carrying newborns on their back, on their chest, in their arms. What Almarina sees that she should not have on the Balkan route, so I hold Almarina's hand tight, to remind her of the baseless hope of children. Because when you walk in a herd it takes nothing to feel like a herd. A boy with an orange hat plays a violin, another opens Google Maps on his phone and caresses Europe. They run across the fields of Slovenia, around a parish church, wearing blankets over their coats, scarves over their chadors. The soldiers wear black and block the road, but the Balkan soldier has his war to tell to the refugee. The netting runs along the border and is forty kilometres long: only those who risk the forest, the mud, the night make it through. On that line is a house: it's inhabited by an old couple who had seen no other migration but that of ducks, and have only seen a postman cross their fields maybe once or twice a year. Helena and her husband live inside, they have been farmers all their life. They let people in one at a time, to take a hot shower. Without stopping, from 6 a.m. until midnight, Helena weaves the dream of letting them all clean up, of being the rain over the cyclamens, the thousand cyclamens in the field before her eyes. In those same days a man comes by, looking for a doctor in the farmers' house: his wife has given birth to their first child.

And because it's almost midnight, I stand up, I remove the batting covering Baby Jesus from the manger, then I switch the nativity scene lights off and I also go to sleep.

When we got back to Nisida, it was floating.

The guards at the barrier looked into my car, and I showed them the magistrate's guardianship authorisation: I was already changing; we had already changed. I was no longer the teacher (outside work hours I was nobody) and she was my daughter on a holiday permit, my almost redeemed and saved daughter, who will have served her full sentence by February. I was bringing her back; they were lifting the barrier. At the first turn in the road I was washed over by abandonment. The wave came and went and would break and leave me soaked, and night had already fallen, and large floodlights like those in commercial ports illuminated the road and made the armoured doors shine. And because I wasn't the teacher but a car dropping off an inmate, that wide mouth swallowed us whole, car and all, and the handover happened there, between one hatch and the other. In the sealed chamber of abandonment, sitting waiting in the car, with me twisted towards the back seat to fetch her bag of nothing and the new suitcase of clothes and food and books and things of mine that she liked, Almarina spoke to me.

'Can't you let me know if Arban is well and where he is? I won't go looking for him when I get out, I promise. I think about the evening when we left. After mum died if I stayed at home my dad would kill me, kill me dead, so my grandma said enough, as soon as the neighbour leaves I'll put you into the lorry with your brother too. I think he's going to school now, don't you think? I think so. And then we crossed the field at night and we thought that dad might kill her too but my grandma told me don't worry, I have one of these, the thing, what's it called in Italian I don't know? The thing you use for grass on top of the staff, like a moon. Yes, a scythe, and we watched my grandma disappear back there in the countryside, on foot, all in black with a scythe in her hands. It's horrible when you don't know if you'll ever see someone or not and then everything else, but at least the journey was nice to begin with, we took the roads by day and we ate the fruit gums that old women sold in baskets and then we'd stop in hostels at night, we'd use the bathroom and that sort of thing. It was after Calafat that we got lost, the neighbour left us, I had to go with the men and that sort of thing, but I still managed to bring him to Italy, Arban I mean, and we stayed together until Fano station and they took us to the police and then they split us up there. But I ran away from the centre to go and find Arban, yes I also stole some things and I ended up here. Can you let me know that Arban is doing okay?'

And *here* was where the gates were already opening and she left with the guard and then the gates closed and I left.

It was a night like any other outside in the celebrating city and as I headed back, in heavy traffic, I had to keep looking at the people in the other cars and tell myself 'They know nothing about how I feel, they see me and think that I'm okay. So I am a little okay. I'm the same as I was on the way there. I'm the same as the other days.' And I told myself so at every traffic light, all the way home.

'You can't, you just can't.' Aurora wipes her mouth with a paper towel. It's the 31st, the year changes tonight, everything changes tonight and to avoid a heavy stomach we're eating fried pizzas in Forcella, *D'e' Figliole*.

'It's the same story, every time. They find them, process them and find out they have no documents, or maybe they do but only because a slightly savvier parent shoved them down their pants, sewed them on to their clothes. OK?'

'OK.'

'So what are they?'

'What are they.'

'Unaccompanied foreign minors. Arban was very young, they definitely found him a family immediately.'

'But why did they split them up?'

'A variety of reasons: better individual chances, in this case the age gap is pretty big, the girl is practically an adult, the other one is very eligible for a family. Because she already had a horrifying life to forget. It's up to the judge. Do you understand?'

'No, I don't, it feels inhumane. But anyway, why can't she see him now?'

'Because I think he's doing okay, they told her the truth: it's better for him this way.'

'And for her? Did anyone think of her, Aurora?'

'We're thinking of her in a different way, Nisida is taking care of her, we are taking care of her.'

'It's not natural; this authority is against nature. It's her brother.'

'That means fuck all. Do you know how many times when everything was going great, these kids had bloomed again and then the smallest contact with their past just dragged them back to old ways?'

'It's her brother.'

'Hang on, let me grab a beer and I'll explain it. It's a matter of paradoxes, if you like. State and Person. Which is right?'

'The Person.'

'You don't think that. You don't, because you pay taxes,

you get paid, you get angry if there's an illegal valet, and you threw away the paper just then in the recycling bin and not on the floor like these troglodytes . . .'

'Don't be like that.'

'Pre-Mesopotamians, is that better? Babylonians already followed the Code of Hammurabi.'

I look around, I look at the Pre-Mesopotamians. I think that they're ignorant, I think that for every child someone like Aurora has, they have seven, I think that they're ruining my city with their haughtiness, and my country with their blind votes. I think that I'm a captive of wise guys, captive of violent guys, of those who have strength but no reason. I think they think that the only possible emancipation from the shit surrounding them is through money, and I think that some don't even realise they live surrounded by shit. I think that the country is full of them, but I also think it's my fault. Mine in the sense of ours, it's our fault. I think that social responsibility is enormous and we are the ones who carry it, the ones who throw the greasy pizza paper in the right bin. I think that there are people like them in every city, but in other cities you don't see them as much because neighbourhoods have separate lives, and if teachers go out for some fried pizza it's like heading out on a safari, whereas here we're all living together: the gate is open and we all keep stepping through it. We're sitting on the same short wall, eating the same pizza, and we only barely agree about basic things: children, for example, or that if it's raining you have to bring in the washing. That summers are hot. I'm a little afraid of them and a little in awe of them.

When I watch them from my balcony, at night, hanging around their scooters until late, making garbled sounds, without realising it's midnight, I realise that they'll never see the mural we painted for them at the yellow gardens, they'll never see in the maths we've explained to exhaustion the plane that will take them away. That they'll never listen to jazz music. And I feel angry and sad, so I head back to bed and at night I'm actually happy to hear them talk. Because as long as they're talking they aren't dealing, they aren't fighting, where there are words there are no knives. And if they can't talk downstairs from my place where can they talk? What other choice do they have, if I'm the only one who will not call the police or throw a bucket of water at them?

'What the fuck does all this have to do with fried pizza? We're talking about something enormous here. We're saying that a sister cannot see her brother because the law said so.'

'But that's your law. So who's right?'

'Almarina.'

'So are the *camorristi* also right? What I mean is if I go and shoot my brother's killer instead of reporting him, am I in the right?'

'Why do you always have to exaggerate, Jesus? Fried pizza first, killers for hire now, what do they have to do with anything? The State can be right and can be wrong. Sometimes it takes ten years to recognise it was wrong, and sometimes to recognise who was right takes us fifty years. Meanwhile people grow up, change, die. We move fast and justice moves slowly.'

'I know. You need to be patient. The Sybil writes her oracle on palm leaves but then the leaves are mixed up by the wind blowing from a hundred cracks. We need to rearrange the message. Leaf by leaf. In any case, if you want to know, Pierluigi will be in Nisida on the morning of the 2nd: the girls have some work to finish in the workshop.'

'Before Nisida, I was unable to tell the difference between a soup bowl and a toilet bowl,' says Pierluigi, and he does so to say that if you really want something, you put the effort in and learn. And you can learn at sixty, too, like he did, as he became my pass.

('We can say I need to help you with the delivery and I'll come with you on the morning of the 2nd, OK?'

If someone, in the glassy air of the start of the year, wants to go into a prison, there must be a reason.

There is no need to explain anything to Pierluigi, there is no need to explain how things really are to many people, actually. Just a small excuse, a veil dimming the shine of truth just a little, so that the glare doesn't blind you.

'I'm not a detective, am I? I'm a retired man who does some volunteering . . .')

So he drove me up. And I sat down in the warm workshop to wait for the girls to come down as he showed me the sets of plates they had to hand in by the 6th.

'It's an important order so we couldn't miss the deadline. It's a guy living in Germany getting married: he came home for Christmas and he's leaving on the 6th. He chose Nisida because he spent his teenage years in here too, and then he left and made his fortune abroad but he's still very attached to the place. Honestly, I couldn't let the kids lose the order and the eight hundred euros. And look, look at how beautiful these are . . .'

He slides the plate across his hands before he passes it to me: it's diamond-like, it looks as though it's only just left the sea. The plates dart in the girls' hands, under Pierluigi's watchful eyes. They're mud coloured, with a palm leaf in the centre. The marks carved into them come from a deep consciousness; Almarina takes me to look at a picture she made with her cellmate. At the end of the day they're tired and happy, they look like small working women after the bell, except that instead of filing back home, they head back to their cells.

I behaved as if nothing was a big deal and I kissed Almarina on her cheek with a loud smack, and to avoid favouritism, I kissed the others too.

One day, Aurora assigned a short Italian essay. The kids had finished and she'd taken the work into the room we use to make coffee, where everything is locked up. The kids are still kids after all. They steal our pens from the class registers, even if they have a jar full of them in class, and for a chance on a mobile phone they will inflict injury. They slip cigarettes out of our pockets though they could just ask, and they probably already have some. They're kids, they're playing, and like kids they love forbidden spaces, and nothing is forbidden here in Nisida. Except for our pockets, sometimes, and the staffroom because that's where we keep paperwork. Inside, locked up inside, is the lined paper that Aurora had handed out, pulling it from the centre of a large notebook, and inside certain memories from that day are preserved. *Something that happened to me when I was small*, was the title of the essay, because in prison there is no talk of the present, and no one can imagine the future. And so all of us – maths teachers and literacy educators included – we all ended up in small houses not too far away from here, just over on the mainland. We stepped into courtyards, we crossed small alleys leading on to large roads on the outskirts. We walked along those roads, kilometres of walls of tall estates, kilometres without a bus stop and where buses don't even run, there's maybe a garage here and there, and a cheese shop, and two possible directions: come home and tell yourself the day is over, or keep going towards whatever the road may bring.

Those who think of Nisida as an aberration don't know the city, and those who think of the city as an aberration don't know the country. This is why the kids are alienated when they first reach Nisida: they see up close, for the first time, adults radically different from those who gave birth to them. It takes nothing for them to acknowledge they've ended up in prison: two days of shock and it's over. They start sleeping again, they pick up this new rhythm that others have talked about; this possibility was made clear during their long games. It takes them much longer to understand this much: that they can trust.

Aurora has that stone face that inmates themselves carve, you never know how she's actually feeling. She's a practical woman, if you need her she's there but you never see her otherwise, she doesn't shirk her duty but she never volunteers either. She's the one who makes the decisions among us. So she studies us while we read the essays or she apologises for having shown them to us, or she thinks that she shouldn't have asked for that memory because she's been there for thirty-five years to add punctuation, not provide psychoanalysis. No one can tell what Aurora thinks of those memories of others that have become our own.

I was small when my dad was released I lived in a small house with my sister and my mum, one day coming home from school where I was in 4 year and my sister started middle school, my mum came to get us in panic telling us to be quick because it was late but it wasn't all true. Because as I walked up the road to our house I saw my dad come out on a stretcher getting on to the first aid, that day was a heavy day because the next day coming home I saw my aunt and my mum telling me that my dad was dead.

V.P.

I remember my father who unfortunately has been in prison for 13 years I was 7 years old we went on the boat with all my family which is my mum and my two brothers we had an amazing day it's the only memory I have left of my father because he's missing for a long time then I have no memories of else because I was small I still get emotional remembering him I hope a day not too far I can have more days like that one.

M.P.

I remember that when I was small I liked spending time with my grandmother, I was 6–7 years old and I wanted her to come to my home or me to go to hers. My grandmother grew me, her personality is very different from me. Even now my grandmother is the person I care the most about, when I started my first incarceration she never came to see me, she started coming to see me halfway through my second incarceration and I really missed her but now I'm happy because I can spend one hour a week with her which means a lot to me.

P.G.

I remember the first day I met my mother: I was more or less 13 years old I was in a foster home; the thing that I remember the most is that they told me 'here, this is your mother' I was frozen for a second, then I went to my bedroom and I got a photo of her, and I told her 'You're not my mother!' I said with anger, spite and hatred towards her, I was so angry I spat in her face. I still feel bad about my actions. The most important thing is that after a few years I made up with her. And now I love her because I was lucky to know that I have a mother because there are many people who have never met them.

E.F.

When I asked the tutor to talk to social services, they told me that social services already had a plan for Almarina.

'But they don't know that I have this availability, they can't know because I've just realised I have it, I just decided I want to try.'

'This isn't just about you, it's about her too, she's a Catholic, they're sending her to don Valentino . . .'

'I know: I took her to Christmas Mass. Can't we ask her what she prefers?'

And the tutor is very patient and very kind – she sometimes stays behind to talk to the girls on the majolica benches when they have doubts about the present or too many certainties about a fixed tomorrow. I trust her, she came back to me with an answer.

'Do you know what she told me, Aurora? Did you hear what they told her? *A single person cannot take care of a girl with a lot of issues.* That's what she said, that a single person can't do much. So what, is don Valentino married?'

'Don't be an idiot, don Valentino is a community, an institute, a centre.'

'It wasn't my choice to be a widow.'

'I know, but it's not something against you, it's a principle.'

'And what are principles good for, can you tell me? Who do they help?'

'They need to start somewhere, darling. Don't get hung up on this, there's a lot to do in here.'

*

I didn't immediately realise that Almarina was no longer here. We don't immediately understand things that hurt us. I didn't realise I would never see her again. I realised other things: that she hadn't come down to the classroom, so I thought she might be busy with the workshops and I thought I might ask about her after the lesson.

Before we go to class, we take the list of the people attending that day from the staffroom: we need to take something that looks like a register, because sometimes orders change in the middle of the night, or over the weekend, and school paperwork is the last thing to be updated.

So there have been weeks when we've never seen the boys, after a fight, but then they come back and they sit in different groupings and look at each other with hatred. They feel their lives waiting for them outside, where they will settle their scores, and they know they just need to wait for this time to be over. Maybe they soften up in the meantime: Ciro, who's constantly doing the wrong thing, is desperately in love with the kitchen lady. He praises her in front of everyone, introducing her as you would a family member: 'D'you see how this kitchen shines, huh, whass she like this woman, be honest? Better'n a mum.' And she looks up from the pots she's washing, filled with pride, and smiles at us.

The kids have a lot of chores, and they do them all. School is the thing that bores them the most, everything else, no matter what it is, they like doing it. First place goes to sport, but so does preparing the boxes for the Community of Sant'Egidio: filling the foil trays, piling them up, sending them out with the list of items in the boxes. Taking care of canteen service, and cooking. The kids love cooking, the boys more than the girls. There's a good pizza oven in Nisida, a brick oven, and Almarina loves putting the pizzas in, so I thought she might be there, sorting out the larger pieces of wood at the back, pulling forward some of the embers.

But she had left: the judge had struck a week off her sentence and she'd packed her suitcase at dawn and headed off to don Valentino. It was good news. It should've been good news: everyone was sure that the Romanian girl would not fall back into crime, and that she would happily finish school because her marks were good, and that don Valentino would slowly teach her how to move in the world without being hurt. It was good news and I heard of it from the captain's eyes, by accident, after peering in vain into every workshop, into the theatre founded by Eduardo de Filippo.

'Fucking bastards,' I told his dark blue eyes staring at me in silence. And I ran away, and if it had been a film he would've chased after me, calling my name, but no.

I called the director from the Coroglio terrace, and he told me all the details of her release.

'Miss, there are two things here: you either trust life and let her go, or you find yourself a lawyer if you want to ask for authorisation to visit her or to go down any other avenue. In any case, jurisdiction over her life is now back in the hands of the judge, and to talk to the judge you need lawyers. That's the extent of what I can tell you, though I hope you'll let it go. In any case, I'll see you in school in the next few days.'

From the Coroglio terrace, Nisida is perfectly aligned with its jetty, and there it is, its lights shining into the daylight-saving evening. Like any vessel, it is unaware of its own crew. It only cares that its hull is intact and devoid of leaks, and those who disembark are no longer its concern. When we were younger we'd look at it for hours, just like now, because this is a romantic spot, where you come to kiss, and if it's late and you have a car and know how to park it, you can even go further. During the day, on the clearing opposite, a nurseryman drives up to sell geraniums and bougainvillea. He might come here because he doesn't have a licence, or maybe because it's a pretty spot, a beautiful spot, a moving spot. It's half the height of Posillipo, the promontory of the wealthy, but still high enough to be dominant over the beach and for you to look at the seagulls circling beneath you. From here, maybe, the future of the city departs, as Rome's fleet once did. The nurseryman watches the bank, and when evening comes, as now, he puts the plastic planters back into his Ape and leaves. The lovers arrive, or those who need to fight (the bar is a little further or a little back, the solution is a little further or a little back), and those who look to the horizon when they need a compromise. One which isn't defined in between things, which isn't raised in the sky nor slammed to the ground, which isn't cloud or factory by necessity. We couldn't even imagine, when we'd come here to kiss, that the inside of Nisida was a prison. Or maybe we did, but we didn't know what a prison was.

I see the lights turn on in the kitchen, and someone touches my shoulder and I almost die.

'. . . the fuck are you doing here?'

'I'm an officer, aren't I?'

'. . .'

'I'm joking, I finished my shift and saw your car on the way up. You know that if you leave it unlocked they'll get in and drive off.'

'. . .'

'I've seen you like this before. For the boy who wanted to take part in the maths olympics. For the one who'd drunk bleach, and for the Senegalese girl. And like you, I've seen many others. It pains me too when one of the kids leaves when I'm not on shift and I don't have a chance to say goodbye. But that's how it is, and this time at least we should be happy, there was no serious offence and there isn't a family out there forcing her back into crime, and because don Valentino is the only priest I know that has understood that the real mission is here. He's a missionary here. So you have to be happy.'

'This time is different.'

'Because you had her over for Christmas?'

'No, because I grew up, captain, I can't fit through Alice's little door any more.'

Don Valentino's centre is in beautiful Pozzuoli. You can walk to it from Nisida, you just need some willpower in your legs. Around you are people running and oblivious with music in their ears, and school children, and people fishing on the rocks, indifferent.

I already know the first answer. So I avoid asking its question and I instead ask to see don Valentino directly; I leave my name, the capacity in which I'm there, I'm told to come back later. To avoid dying again I head towards the archaeological site to lose myself among the Germans, among the guides and their tiny umbrellas, and the Japanese groups listening to their earpieces. In the distance, everywhere, is a hint of spring. In the temple of Mercury, students are looking at a fig tree that grew upside down. One of the girls asks for an explanation, but the teacher accompanying them is only an art expert, and the others don't really care. So I move closer and I talk to her and her alone.

'The roots are in the tuff, fig trees can do this, they latch on to the rock and resist draughts because they suck out the water still in the rock. Now, this tree would like to head upwards like the others, because the leaves seek out the sunlight, right? But what little life was left in the sprig that generated it, what little sap is left in the roots, well, this is the hole it found to come out. There was no way up, so it headed downwards. And look at the magnificent tree.'

'It's even prettier, I think, because it's different from all the other ones, if I see a normal fig tree I don't want to take a picture.'

As her teacher, a little worried, calls to her, she looks at me.

Her eyes are yellow. She watches me as she heads back to her classmates, wearing jeans and a stripy rucksack, her skin shining in the sun – as though she's the source of an ancient, meridian light. She leaves me with the smile of revelation and, the moment she exits the cave, she disappears.

*

'Miss, what you've done isn't right: I'm meeting you because you teach at the prison, but you come here as a ordinary person asking to see one of the guests and you know better than me that to see the guests you need authorisation.'

'Don Valentì, what do you need me to do? Pretend I'm confessing? Should I kneel down and talk to you through a grate? All I want to know is, if I were to file a fostering request for Almarina, would you be pleased? Should I try or not? I need to know, c'mon.'

You don't immediately recognise when your life is about to change. Along with the movement we give to it, we do not immediately recognise the change. It takes me forever. Intentionally or not, I notice the new stream only once I'm in it. And even if I know its origin, I cannot see its end. I become aware of parts of me only through mirrors, looking at photos from the past, even the recent past, and I study myself as if that were another person, which she is. Action is one step ahead of awareness, and that's why I booked an appointment with the lawyer and I went and told her everything and it was only in the glass lift in Chiaia, only then, that I realised I had actually done it. I signed a proxy on the side of a document, meaning that I gave a woman the task of moving into the world for me and for Almarina. When I reached the ground floor, I wanted to call my husband, or my mother. (They had those old orange phones in the faculty cloister, you'd slot in a few coins and you'd call 'How did it go?' '28 out of 30' 'Well done'.) I missed that phone call, so I walked through the alleys and slipped into a Sri Lankan shop, one with Arabic and English and those characters that look like embroidery on the glass door. I left my ID at the desk in exchange for a place. All the languages of the world around me, each in their own compartment, each on their own chair, headset and microphone and screen turned on, sitting women and men and children throwing hopes and anger to the other side of the world, and reassurances and questions too.

'Antonio, listen, I'll never forgive you for leaving me alone with the notary the day we agreed on the mortgage with the bank, because the notary pointed out things and I was embarrassed. But I am sorry I never let you put the TV in the living room, in front of the sofa, yes.'

And because the Sri Lankan guy at the entrance was watching me, I even called my sister-in-law, the least ugly one, and invited myself to her place for lunch on Sunday.

I turn on the TV, I leave the blinds open, I'm starting to enjoy this relaxed rhythm. And if I'm starting to enjoy it it's because Antonio's ghost has definitely left me. I leave the blinds open and he loved the dark, I watch TV in bed and he hated any type of screen at night. After three years of loneliness I am finally alone and not abandoned, I reclaim the spaces which the soul of who used to fill them has slowly returned to me. What used to make me suffer has become sweet, and he's become a deeper part of me, one that can no longer be reflected in mirrors or echo in footsteps across the room. I'll always miss him but this missing is no longer a painful thorn: it wooed me, and I can truly fall asleep in the middle of a double bed, stretching out each limb like the Vitruvian man, and swim across the sheets, become square and round without betraying anyone.

At dawn, barefoot and in my pyjamas, I open the door to a woman who asks me who I am before she tells me who she is. Then tells me, tersely:

'Social services.'

I was waiting for and fearing her, and when she shows up her shape is that of a woman I usually pity. Yellow, not blond, dyed hair, cheap but showy clothes, too much lipstick for that time of day. A barefoot teacher judging a bold clerk, and a dyed clerk judging on paper a sloppy teacher.

'Coffee?'

'I couldn't, thank you.'

'I'm making it for myself.'

'Oh, OK then.'

She follows me to the kitchen.

'Can I take a look around?'

'Please, be my guest.'

She turns her back to me and I switch on the boiler, I push the box with the empty bottles into a corner with my feet: on top of them all is the shiny blue gin bottle, and my heart expands.

'Sugar?'

When we sit down again she pulls out a pre-filled form. Question answer box question answer box question answer box, then some ancient handwriting, female, of someone who stopped there.

After adding the date, I'm folded up and put back into her bag, along with my home and the coffee cup I'm holding in my hands.

When the portly handmaid is already halfway down the stairs, ready to deliver her oracles of worthiness, I add a splash of sambuca to my life and to my coffee.

Sometimes people are used to dealing with hospitals, and other times with lawyers. People who grow older get used to dealing with graveyards, almost always. These are horrible places, where you constantly feel uncomfortable, places of the world where our existence has become stranded and we can't wait to rev up the motor and get out of them as quickly as possible. Later, with time, we'll talk about it or avoid thinking about it. But I'm fairly confident about the statistics when I claim that very few people have to deal with both prison and youth court. It's not something that just happens to you. I asked for prison the day I listed Nisida as third choice for my teaching appointment. Third choice, but still a choice, and a likely one at that. What brought me to youth court was the human condition.

From a personal perspective, it was worse than prison. Because everything's already decided in prison, whereas in front of the judge, anything can happen. And there's a rational side to which you anchor yourself, the one that says that the law is all written down, you just need to remember it well, understand it, and there will be no mistakes. But there is also a deeper aspect, a fathom into the heart of darkness (if there is no bottom, an anchor is useless) where your entire destiny, your life, what your days will be like and how much strength you'll have are up for discussion. Someone else will discuss it, the shape it will have taken in their mind, the variables you weren't able to explain or that the forms didn't allow you to explain, that lovely dream that the law hasn't yet written out, or not like that. Your life, essentially, won't really be represented in front of the judge, they won't really be able to imagine it. There will be some other shape in their mind that's not only not entirely accurate, but also so different from your actual case (your entire existence, the entirety of your future and that of your loved ones), the eventual solution, the judgement, the sentence, which will tell an entirely different story.

Because you need a lot of time, or a perfect poem, to say how things truly are.

And hearings are short, and appeals aren't written in verse. So there is one gigantic effort needed not to believe you depend entirely on the rhetorical skills of a lawyer, as if it were a religion. A single effort to make to avoid dying of fright or starting to hate every gowned person who isn't you and who will decide for you (hate is a constant gangrenous fear, a defence become misunderstanding, a cry remained too long at the centre of the earth and which no one has heard in time). You need to step into their skin. The skin of those of you who judge. We need to reach across to you, cross the space that sets itself as border without actually being one, but which still exists everywhere, in court, in classrooms, in parliament. We need physically to go, move, cross the square; don't allow it to be divided into those protesting and those who think they're defending it, because there is nothing to defend. You need to move into the courts, climb the stairs, physically, feel them in your legs. You need to swim to the territorial border to realise that one stroke over it's still just water, and the sea is the same, and there is no border. There is no border. There is no prison: Nisida vanishes like a ghost ship, in the exact moment that Mariela starts working with don Valentino, and Paolo takes his wife and son and heads north, to start again where no one knows him. We need to come closer to those of you who judge. Cross the grey room, meeting that grey as if it were the most vivid of colours, telling yourself that during the same years that I was studying maths you were studying the law, that we've had similar joys, similar troubles, and have loved the same musicians during the same stupid years. Rip apart that initial divide in which we so believed: that you become teachers, or prisoners, or artists, or judges because we're different on the inside. Because that's exactly where we're the same. I learned something, standing in court, that has nothing to do with the sentence. I learned that just as when I assign something in class it's not because the syllabus tells me to, I shape it, I sharpen it, I articulate it in what I think's the best way for the kids to be able to use their critical skills; and it's the same for the judges, they don't do what they do because they think it's right. They do it because justice is a possible conclusion of a reasoning. And I think it must be difficult to mark that decision: that the girl can come and live with me for as long as she wants.

So I did what I always do, as I did before my biology exam: I jump into the water. There was no one else around. I left all my clothes there, under lido Pola, and I went in naked. The coast is born from the corpses of the abandoned steelworks, it sharpens to the left under the Coroglio promontory with its tuff alcoves, and to the right it opens into Pozzuoli. Before me, only Nisida.

If you wish for Nisida to set sail, you need to untie the sailor's knot that moors it to its regal city, if you want to be free, you need to feel free. And because the current was strong that day, because it was only early April, I held myself steady with my knees in the sand. That's how I prepared tomorrow's speech.

Epilogue

Halfway up the Colli Aminei I see Aurora and Pierluigi step off the 178.

'We're really hurt you didn't make us your witnesses.'

'You owe us breakfast.'

In the courts, we focus on our surroundings to make sure we have the right room, just as when we go to vote.

'Earrings look good on you,' says the director, from further up the stairs, and those earrings are my wedding rings.

He's smoking next to a window, with the captain, and I realise I've never seen the captain in his uniform, and I'm surprised that it's not a white sailor uniform. But what surprises me the most is that they're both smoking.

'Did you both just start?'

'I only smoke when I'm nervous, I never buy them. The director has always smoked.'

'I've never seen you holding a cigarette.'

'I smoke in secret, when I'm in Nisida . . .'

I see him for the first time as he heads down the scarp leading to the crater, down the cone's spine to Porto Paone, after the kids have headed back to the buildings, and passes by the remains of General Bellomo; and the captain's dog goes ahead of him because the dog is the owner here and the owner has a great responsibility. I see him as it gets dark, between the pines over the purple water, and I finally understand what those hidden glints at any given cell window are. I reply to the captain.

'And why are you nervous? This is court stuff, your sort of stuff.'

'First of all because I don't know how to speak in the way that you all speak and I don't want to say anything wrong, and then it's important for you and for us, because if it goes as it should you'll calm down a little and we'll all feel better . . . I even wore my uniform to make a good impression.'

'Idiot.'

But then, while the director and Aurora and Pierluigi chat, he holds me close in the way that a man holds a woman.

Just like that, it'll happen here, in the grey room, while Almarina can sort of see me through the crack in the door (she's wearing the Madonna del Buon Consiglio pendant that her grandma gave her). It'll happen here, viale dei Colli Aminei, 42, third floor, last room on the right, here is where you'll decide whether our clothes will mix in the wash: dark with dark and whites with whites. Whether I'll add chillies to the olive and caper sauce or not.

Under the coat, behind the binders, lawyer standing, you will decide whether I will hear the lift come to my floor and steps moving towards my door. Whether 4 GBs of data a month will be enough, how long I'll have to wait for the bathroom, whether we'll be going to Elba this summer or if Procida will do.

My name is Elisabetta Maiorano, I was born in Naples in the 1900s and I hope I'll soon be out of here, out of this place of judgement. This place of summaries, where our two lives, a total of around seventy years, two countries, a stretch of sea where our dead rest, are condensed into a few pages processed by the records office. We will never be able to tell you fully what our retinas have retained, nor what, of those images, has changed our hearts forever. Because we're women in progress, and when we step out of here we'll already be different.

The road to Nisida is long and uphill, and holding everything together is an effort, and doing everything right is impossible. And so, absorbed by daily tasks, I had forgotten the love of a mother on the steps of the ancient home, where memories stay in our absence: undeserved, unrequited, unconquered.

When we talked at don Valentino's in Pozzuoli (because yes, we did talk, quietly, walking around the cloister, and then sitting on the almost five-hundred-year-old majolica bench, still there, still with its colours painting hunting scenes), Almarina told me something that made me understand that she really wanted me to take her home. She told me: 'I can't promise you anything.'

My name is Elisabetta Maiorano, I can only remember my PIN because I found a mathematical relation between the digits, I live in Naples and I hope. And I can't stop: I wake up and I hope, and this is the only reason why I don't fear judgement. There's another reason too: what can I possibly be afraid of, after I have been judged by the eyes and actions of the inmates, backwards and forwards in that suspended classroom. Those who have crossed the gaze of incarcerated youth have already passed, all that's left is to step towards the future. If Almarina will ever have the chance to go abroad, I want to take her to Paris, I want to give her an end-of-school trip, no exams, no school. No marks: because that's what my husband and I were looking for, it's what people who don't stop for what life gives them are looking for. A different term to adhere to.

Then we'll go back to Romania, I promised her that. We'll go back to its strange buildings, the composite squares, where history hasn't had time to stratify. It's just piled up in its styles, in the painted-over Soviet houses. We'll go back to Bucharest, under the knots that hold its cables, among sage-coloured walls, among the streets of the shopping centres and the streets still made of mud: we'll go to look for Almarina's mother. We will go to look for her together and at her tomb I will show her just how far Almarina has walked just to come back. We will listen, in silence, as one does in graveyards. And she will ask us about Arban, of course, and we will tell her that he's well, he's eating, he's studying, he sleeps in a warm bed and wears clean clothes, and one day he'll also come back. And for this sentence to be true, we will look for Arban a little every day, we'll look for him in the papers, in the archives, in computers. We'll look for him in foster homes and families and homes and if you won't let us see him, we will look. We will spy on his games through the window and we'll leave a rose and a lizard on the windowsill.

Because there is something that eludes you all, and no one will say it out loud, so I will: love doesn't recognise authority. Formally, yes, we're forced to recognise it: but inside our bones, when we check our wrinkles in the mirror, or the truth in our sleep, we do not give you the right to decide. That way no one is on a special list, no one lives apart. We follow you into this paper world, pushed back every so often and propelled forwards just the same, like those tiny metal marbles in plastic toy labyrinths. We follow you with a single fixed point in front of us: when we have found the door leading back to sea, we will burn all this paper, and the fire will warm us up.

It'll be a glorious bonfire, you'll see: we'll set it up in piazza Mercato, and the pyre will be the tallest ever seen. There will be forms and incomes and family status and citizenship rights; and police records and attachments, warnings and regulations and tax records and evictions. And, if you want, we'll throw your gowns on there too. Sex workers will teach us how to make the spark that sets everything ablaze and at that moment you'll see it shine on the coast long before reaching Capri. Millions of numbers taken in waiting rooms will rise into the air, giving us back the time we waited for. That way, there will be enough to dispel all fear and cold for the rest of the night: until the rise of a new day, still far away.

(When we met in Pozzuoli, Almarina baffled me. She was wearing fuchsia, the only fuchsia dress I had in the wardrobe and which she immediately fell in love with, so I gave it to her even though I thought it was too grown up. But when we tightened the belt, it really showed off her hips. 'I thought I might buy a headband' – her hair was already shoulder length. She took me to see the monastery's medicinal herbs, and there I realised that there was still an entire future to be had. Not mine, nor ours: I mean hers. I'm saying that I saw the woman she would become because she was already all there, she was getting ready, she was getting ready to be born again. Outside me, far from her past, beyond the human sickness that hurt her, Almarina walks up and down the metro to university, to the chemistry department, her loafers on the escalator, then in the classrooms, in the labs, among fellow students who cannot know what was there before. She's quick to learn the botanical names, because it's the same as Latin: it was already there, in her mother's voice, and who could have thought? But one day she recognised it in the name of moss and of honeysuckle, she found it again in the depths of the forest that saw her escape. In the root of the words that she had to stop speaking as a young girl were the university herbals. It may have been chemists' balms or witching potions, but from within the body of Almarina bound, free Almarina emerged. My geometry professor, after all, always said that you need to point the compass somewhere first to see how big a circle you can draw, and Almarina is right there, right in the centre.)

Author's Acknowledgements

For the stories: Michele Rossi, Grazia Ofelia Cesaro, Imma Pascucci. For Nisida: Maria Franco and Gianluca Guida. For the sisterhood: Le patate – year I.

May this book, as a paper flower, reach those who did not stay quiet: Caterina D'Ambrosi, Marina Saviano, Nicola Lagioia and Nicola Oddati; also Teresa Ciabatti, Elisa Fuksas, Giovanna Cau and Matilde Cascone.

Translator's Acknowledgements

To Jonathan Lee, of the ERRC, for the consultation. To Valeria, for answering the silliest, most basic questions. To E, for listening to me reading this book out loud several times over several months.